RO' TRIP

By Holly Kowitt

Based on "Ro' Trip"
Written by Thomas W. Lynch
A Tom Lynch Company Production

SCHOLASTIC INC.

New York   Toronto   London   Auckland   Sydney
Mexico City   New Dehli   Hong Kong   Buenos Aires

No part of this work may be reproduced in whole or in part, stored in a retrieval system, or transmitted in any form or by any means, electronic, mechanical, photocopying, recording, or otherwise, without written permission of the publisher. For information regarding permission, write to Scholastic Inc., Attention: Permissions Department, 557 Broadway, New York, NY 10012.

ISBN 0-439-89041-1

Published by Scholastic Inc.
SCHOLASTIC and associated logos are trademarks and/or registered trademarks of Scholastic Inc.

12 11 10 9 8 7 6 5 4 3 2 1   6 7 8 9 10/0

Printed in the U.S.A.
First printing, September 2006

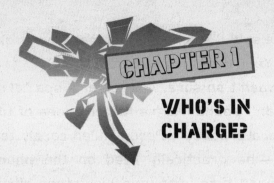

CHAPTER 1

WHO'S IN CHARGE?

Romeo and Louis Miller clomped down the stairs, loaded with suitcases. As soon as they saw Angeline off, they'd be parent-free for a whole week. Romeo couldn't wait.

"This is going to be the greatest spa weekend of our lives," announced Angeline, Romeo's stepmother. She and Percy, Romeo's father, were going away together for the first time since the birth of their baby, Bobby, seven months ago. Nearby, Bobby gurgled happily in his infant seat.

Angeline showed the spa brochure to Gary, Romeo's ten-year-old brother. "A warm honey bath?" he read, wrinkling up his face. "What's *that*?"

Angeline's voice rose with excitement. "It's

incredible," she said. "The honey — it makes your skin look fantastic. Your dad's gonna love it."

Romeo wasn't so sure. A week at a spa taking honey baths didn't sound like his father's idea of fun. As a busy record producer, Percy Miller rarely took time to relax — he practically lived on the phone. Romeo had a hard time imagining his father sitting still long enough for skin treatments.

"Ang, I still don't know how you convinced Dad to go to a spa," said Ro, shaking his head.

"I didn't have to convince him," insisted Angeline. "He's very excited about going."

"Well, of course he is," said Lou with a sigh. "Getting pampered, taking naps, getting pampered again . . ." He plucked the brochure out of Gary's hands. "Where do I sign up?"

To Lou, the trip sounded luxurious. Before being adopted by the Miller family a few years ago, Lou had spent time in different homes as a foster child. Fancy vacations were a novelty to him, and he was still amazed that he was lucky enough to be a part of such a privileged, happy household.

As Lou read aloud from the spa brochure, the

phone rang. Romeo dove for it. "Hello . . . oh, hey, Dad," said Romeo. "I can't believe you're going to a spa." Romeo chuckled, picturing his dad's face covered in honey. "Why?"

Percy's voice crackled on his cell phone. "Is Ang standing there?" he asked.

"Yeah," said Romeo, turning away from his stepmother.

His father sighed. "Tell her I said, cuz *this is going to be the greatest spa week of our lives*," instructed Percy.

Angeline walked over to Romeo excitedly. "What'd he say?" she asked. She was sure Percy was looking forward to this vacation as much as she was.

"'This is going to be the greatest spa week of his life,'" Romeo repeated dutifully. Angie squealed and clapped her hands. He knew his father was trying to please his new wife, whose warmth and good nature had made her an adored member of the family.

Angeline took the phone, and they made arrangements to meet at the airport. "I'm so excited," she said in a low voice. "Thank you for doing this."

"Hey, I want to do it," said Percy. "It's time we

had a nice, romantic vacation. I love you, baby."
Angeline made a kissing sound and hung up the phone,
just as Jodi burst in the door. She was in her first
year of college at the nearby university.

"Jodi, what are you doing home?" asked Romeo,
trying not to scowl. His plans for a parent-free week
hadn't included his older sister.

"Hello to you, too," Jodi said sarcastically, tossing down her backpack and glaring at him.

Angeline intervened smoothly. "Jodi, I'm glad
you're here," she said warmly. "Guys, Jodi's going to
help out with Bobby when I'm gone."

Lou let out a cry of protest. "Ang, on behalf of
me and my brothers, we're insulted that you don't
think we're mature enough to hold down the fort," he
said. After all, they were in high school now. The boys
puffed up their chests to look responsible.

"Yeah," said Gary defiantly. He rushed over to
Lou and Ro to show solidarity, but on his way he
knocked over a glass vase. It crashed to the floor,
exploding into a thousand pieces. Across the room,
Bobby looked up from his fuzzy toys, startled.

"I rest my case," said Angeline sweetly. "You gonna clean that up?"

A horn honked outside. "Oh, there's my taxi," said Angeline. Turning to Bobby, she cooed, "You want to walk Mommy to the taxi?" Jodi scooped up some suitcases and walked out with her stepmother. Gary grabbed some more bags and followed them outside.

"Hey, Ang," Lou shouted after her. "Don't forget to try the saltwater flotation tank — they say it's great for meditation!"

Ro shook his head, trying to imagine Percy meditating. As he reached for a broom, the phone rang.

"I'm looking for Romeo Miller," said a deep voice on the other end of the line. Ro put down the broom. "This is Joe Blanchard, from The Shop."

Romeo almost dropped the phone. Joe Blanchard was the head of one of the hottest record labels in the country! He'd discovered some major R&B and hip-hop acts. It was Ro's dream to get signed by a label like The Shop. A label like that would take their band, The Romeo Show, to a national audience.

He covered the receiver and called Louis over.

"It's the dude from The Shop!" he whispered. "In Los Angeles! The guy I met on the golf course! Joe Blanchard!"

Trying to be cool, Romeo cleared his throat. "Hey, Mr. Blanchard," he said. "What can I do for you?"

"It's what *I* can do for *you*," Joe said smoothly. "Your man Hacksaw sent me your demo. It's good."

Hacksaw was the band's manager. He'd been sending out The Romeo Show's music to producers and agents — anyone who could help them get a recording contract.

Romeo beamed. "Cool, glad you liked it," he said, exchanging glances with Louis.

"Like it?" said Joe. "I love it. That's why I'm sending Wild Wayne Finebaum tomorrow night to check you out live," he said.

Romeo chuckled. "Wild Wayne Finebaum?" he repeated dubiously. What kind of a name was *that*?

"He's my number one A&R guy," said Blanchard. "I know you have the music chops. He's going to see if you can perform. If he likes you, I'll sign you," he said simply. "Good luck, kid."

"Cool," said Romeo, but Joe had already hung

up. Romeo was thrilled that The Shop was seriously interested. In a few short years, The Romeo Show had made a name for themselves around Seattle. But being courted by a major label — *that* was a whole new ball game.

He turned to Louis. "Lou, tomorrow night could be the biggest night of our lives!" Lou was in the band, too, along with Gary. Jodi had also been a band member, until she got too busy with college classes and activities.

"Are you serious?" shouted Lou. They touched fists and did a funky victory dance, moving down the hall in an exaggerated hip-hop stroll.

All they had to do was be brilliant tomorrow night.

No problem.

CHAPTER 2

OH, BABY!

Rehearsing the next day, everyone in the band felt the pressure. They'd spent all afternoon in the Millers' comfortably cluttered garage, which served as the band's rehearsal space.

Everyone was there, including Ashley, the new female vocalist. "You know you come to party/get on your feet," she sang in her silky voice. Wearing a white camisole, sequined scarf, and silver hoop earrings, with her long silky hair hanging down perfectly, she looked too glamorous for the grungy garage.

As the last notes faded away, Lou turned to her. "Ash, you killed it," he exclaimed. She giggled and brushed back her hair. "It feels tight," she agreed.

"Hold up, hold up," said Romeo, putting down the mic. "We're not all *that* tight. Louis, you were playing too fast," he said, pointing to him. He turned to Gary. "And you need to stay on beat. . . ." he said.

"Ex-*cuse* me?" said Louis, exchanging glances with Gary. Since when had Romeo become such a taskmaster? Ro turned to Ashley. "And you . . ." he began. Ashley tossed her long black hair defiantly.

"Yes?" she demanded, stepping up to face him. She lifted her chin, and Ro shifted uneasily.

"Nothing!" he squeaked, with a false laugh. With her good looks and confident manner, Ashley could be intimidating. "Stay focused. Alright, " he said, addressing everyone. "Let's run through it all again."

Ashley didn't budge. "Hang on," she said. "Ro, slow your stroll."

"*Slow my stroll?*" repeated Ro incredulously. "Who says 'slow your stroll'?" he asked.

"I just made it up," said Ashley. She paused for a moment, and spoke in a lower tone of voice. "Ro. The fact is, we sound great. If we give that same performance tonight for Wild Finebaum . . ." She shrugged matter-of-factly. "We're in."

Romeo took a deep breath. It was time to take charge. The band didn't realize what a big deal tonight was. If they got signed by The Shop, they'd get national exposure. They'd play all over the country.

But they wouldn't get signed unless they were drop-dead awesome. Wild Wayne probably checked out bands all the time. If they were anything less than fantastic tonight, he wouldn't waste his time.

"Ash, Lou, Gary," he began. "I don't think you're aware of what's come our way. You see, we have to seize this opportunity." His voice rose and he started gesturing dramatically. "Take it and run up that ladder of success," he intoned.

Gary yawned. Ashley rolled her eyes.

"And if I come off a little strong, it's only because I'm trying to lead us to the promised land!!" Ro's voice got even higher, as if he were preaching a sermon. "Are you with me?" he asked dramatically, still addressing a congregation.

His eyes swept the room. Louis was listening to headphones, thumping his hands to the beat. Ashley was slumped in a corner, filing her nails. Gary was reading a music magazine.

In less than five hours, The Romeo Show would

get a one-time-only shot at the big leagues. So far, the band had developed a great local reputation for their hot rhymes and lush vocals, but this was their chance to become *stars*.

And yet: look at them! They were practically asleep. Didn't they realize this was their breakout moment? Tonight they'd be playing Seattle's hottest club for one of the top people in the music business, not some junior high school prom. They had to be completely focused.

"Is anybody hungry?" asked Louis.

"Starving!" shouted Gary and Ashley together.

"Let's eat," said Gary, tossing his magazine on the keyboard.

Romeo looked at his band mates. "How about the promised land?" he pleaded, watching his band file out of the garage.

"After we eat," said Gary firmly, closing the door.

Romeo shook his head. This crew was hopeless.

Inside the house, Jodi put Bobby in his stroller. "C'mon, Bobby, let's go for your walk," she cooed. The baby looked especially cute today, she thought, in his matching blue cotton cap, coveralls, and booties.

"You're here!" shouted Hacksaw, crashing through the kitchen door. As The Romeo Show's manager, he was a frequent guest at the Miller house. With his long, dark blond hair and excitable manner, Hacksaw always entertained the Millers, bringing flurry to an already tumultuous household.

"Hey, Hacksaw," said Jodi, puzzled by his frantic energy. "Ready for tonight's gig?" she asked.

Hacksaw threw up his hands. "Tonight?" he asked. "Who cares about tonight? I'm about right now," he said passionately. "I am *in the moment*."

Jodi rolled her eyes. "Okay," she said, rattling a set of giant toy keys in front of Bobby. "Can I help you with something?"

"No, not you," said Hacksaw. "But he can," he said, pointing at Bobby dramatically. "Big Bobby Miller . . ." He approached the baby, and leaned down to scoop him up.

Jodi cut him off with her arm. "Don't touch the baby, Hacksaw," she said.

"Right," he said, backing away. "Jodi, I just

received a call from a commercial agent who just had a baby walk out on him," he said excitedly.

"Huh?" asked Jodi, wiping off Bobby's mouth with a washcloth.

"Well, he didn't walk out. He sort of . . . crawled out," Hacksaw explained. "Okay, the point is, Bobby Miller here is eighteen pounds of killer charisma."

Jodi had to agree. Her baby brother was pretty irresistible.

Hacksaw pointed to Bobby with both hands. "Son, you are on the inside track to become the new face of Crandall's Baby Food!" Hacksaw exclaimed.

Bobby looked at Hacksaw and spit up.

Hacksaw turned to Jodi. "What's his schedule like?" he asked, as if the seven-month-old might have a calendar full of appointments. It was clear he was used to dealing with musicians — *not* infants.

"He eats, he sleeps, he poops," listed Jodi. "He gets changed nine, ten times a day . . . and that's about it."

Hacksaw absorbed this. "So he's open," he concluded.

"I guess he is," she said with a shrug.

"But we won't tell them that," said Hacksaw with a wink, pacing around the kitchen. "We'll make 'em think he's in demand." Jodi gave him a questioning look, but his mind was already racing.

Crandall's Baby Food was just a first step, he thought, plotting the baby's career path. Bobby Miller was going to be a star.

At the spa, Angeline and Percy reclined on massage tables in matching white bathrobes. They were blissfully unaware of the tumult back home. Their faces were covered in creamy green paste, and cucumber slices topped their eyelids.

"Ahhh . . . this is so perfect." Angeline sighed. "Thank you, Percy." She loved the feel of the cool cream against her skin, and the fragrance of fresh flowers in a nearby vase. Vanilla-scented candles flickered on the windowsill.

Percy shifted on the table. His back was getting sore. "You don't have to thank me, baby. This is what marriage is all about," he explained. "Two people spending quality time with each other . . ." He drummed his fingers on the table, trying to relax.

She smiled, keeping her eyes closed. "How do you like the lime avocado face mask?" she asked, expecting him to praise the refreshing skin treatment. So far, the spa had been everything she'd hoped for: restful, beautiful, close to nature.

"It's starting to itch, baby," complained Percy. He wasn't used to having stuff on his face. He wished this room had a television in it. The silence was getting on his nerves.

"Try not to think about it," said Angeline, but somehow her words just made him think about it even more. He squirmed, and started to scratch his face.

"Don't scratch it," Angeline instructed without looking at him. She heard his fingers scrape his face. "No, Percy," she pleaded.

But Percy couldn't take it anymore. He leaped off the table and grabbed a towel to wipe off the mask. As he jumped up, cucumber slices slid off his eyes and on to the floor. Wiping the thick green goo off his face was a relief.

Angeline removed the cucumbers from her own eyes and looked at him. "Oh, dear," she murmured. This day was getting off to a rough start.

Percy smiled weakly. He knew it wasn't easy for Angie to keep up her career as an architect, raise an infant, and be a mother to the other four Miller kids. She held the family together with wisdom, humor, and loving attention that never ran out. Didn't she deserve a week off to do whatever she wanted?

She looked so disappointed that he hadn't liked the facial mask. How was he going to tell her that it wasn't just the mask he hated — it was the whole "spa" experience?

Accustomed to the busy life of a record producer, it drove Percy crazy to sit around in a bathrobe with mud on his face. He hadn't checked his messages all day. But this was Angie's dream vacation — he *had* to stick it out.

Percy just didn't know if he could.

CHAPTER 3

BIG NIGHT

It was ten o'clock at night, and Club Scrape was pulsating. With its blue lights and glass bricks, the former warehouse had a spare, gritty look that made it a hot venue for R&B, hip-hop, and house concerts.

In front of the club, Hacksaw paced nervously. As the band's manager, it was his job to greet Wild Wayne Finebaum, A&R man at The Shop. He scanned the crowd for music industry types, who tended to be young, slick, and well dressed.

Instead he spotted Myra, Romeo's neighbor and school friend. With her long, curly blond hair and funky red glasses, she was hard to miss. Hacksaw greeted her eagerly. He needed her to keep Wayne company during the concert.

Hacksaw and Myra chatted, but his eyes kept wandering. Finally, he saw a cool young guy with spiky dark hair, laid back in a striped shirt and black blazer. That was him! He was never wrong about these things.

"Let me guess. You're in the music business, right?" said Hacksaw, practically tackling him.

"You got it," said the guy, pointing his finger at Hacksaw. "I didn't miss the set, did I?" he asked. Myra shook her head. "Sweet. My flight from L.A. was delayed, and I thought I was going to miss the show," he explained.

Myra and Hacksaw exchanged glances of relief. It was Wild Wayne! "Tell you what," said Hacksaw. "We just happen to have a special spot for you right up front," he said, guiding him into the club.

As she followed behind Hacksaw, Myra saw Romeo and Lou peek out from behind the curtain. She smiled broadly and shot them a thumbs-up.

Backstage, Romeo and the gang exploded with excitement. "Wild Wayne's here!" Romeo shouted.

Ashley clutched her stomach. "I just got nervous!" she cried.

Louis agreed. "The butterflies in my stomach

just got butterflies in *their* stomachs," he said, talking rapidly.

Gary started gasping as though he were having a panic attack.

"Gary!" Romeo shook him. "Pull it together." He turned to everyone else. "This is the show that could bring us to the next level," he said in a low voice. "Are you with me?"

Romeo put his fist out. "One, two, three . . ." he counted. "Team!" The others shouted, putting their fists together. They gave each other daps, which had become a pre-show ritual — a last moment of bonding before they went out to face an unpredictable audience.

They scattered onto the stage as a voice announced, "Ladies and gentlemen, please welcome Seattle's own . . . The Romeo Show!" As Gary dropped the first beats, the audience hooted happily for the much-loved band.

Glamorous in a one-sleeved purple blouse, Ashley started off the set. "You know you come to party," she sang. "Get on your feet/I know how you feel/Get used to the beat." The crowd roared their approval.

Romeo blended in smoothly with his rap. "I got the girls trying to read me like a psychic, telling me to dump my Sidekick, let's go out and catch a little right quick. . . ." He could feel the club's energy take him higher and higher.

This was what he lived for: watching the crowd sway back and forth to his rhymes. He waved his arm in the air, feeling the connection with the audience. This moment was pure magic.

He had the crowd rocking — now it was time to make the mood more intimate. "What I know is true love, it disappears," he crooned. "My heart broke again, I wish you was here." The girls in the audience screamed.

Now the lush rhythms grew softer, as Romeo's song turned into a love ballad. "With you to the very end, that's why I wanna make you my girlfriend." Then he brought the energy up again, and rolled out his most irresistible rhymes.

Romeo looked around at his band. Tonight they

were a tightly oiled machine, nailing every song, note by note. Gary was laying down beats that no one could sit still to, while Ashley was singing her heart out. They were on fire.

Their last song was a new number they'd been rehearsing, a show-stopping party jam that brought down the house. The crowd exploded, and Romeo knew it had been one of their fiercest concerts ever.

Down in the front row, the A&R guy turned to Hacksaw. "That was amazing," he shouted, trying to be heard above the roar. "Electric! This band is the hottest thing I've seen in five years!" he said, pointing at the stage.

Hacksaw beamed. "Tell you what," he said. "How'd you like to tell Romeo that yourself?"

Wild Wayne looked thrilled. "I'd love to," he said, looking from Myra to Hacksaw. Myra grinned back, and Hacksaw gave her arm a squeeze. She recognized her cue to run backstage and give the band a heads-up.

Taking Wayne by the elbow, Hacksaw guided him out of the room and into the lobby. He parked him next to a brick wall covered in graffiti. "Wait here," he ordered.

Backstage, Romeo held up his bottled water in a toast to his crew. "To the greatest band mates ever," he proclaimed. "I think we blew Finebaum away," he said. "In fact, I know we did." Everyone laughed and congratulated each other, clinking bottles together with gusto.

Myra appeared suddenly, bursting with excitement. "Ro," she began, trying to catch her breath. "Wayne Finebaum wants to meet you. He loved it." She motioned for everyone to rush out to the lobby. "Come on," she called.

As she ran off, Ro smiled with satisfaction, and relief. Despite the awesome pressure they'd been under, they'd aced the show tonight, and Wayne was blown away. Now The Shop would *definitely* sign them.

Romeo started to race to the lobby, then he slowed himself down. Be cool, he told himself, observing the spiky-haired man from a distance. As he approached, Hacksaw hailed him with an outstretched arm.

"Here comes The Shop's newest superstar act," Hacksaw exclaimed.

Romeo forgot his cool and pumped Wayne's hand eagerly. "Glad you could make it," he said, wiping his brow on his sleeve.

"Not a problem," said Wayne. He turned to Hacksaw. "And thank you for the first-class treatment," he said. "Very unexpected."

Romeo gave a dismissive wave of his hand. "Hey, for you . . . anything," he said. "Right, guys?" Everyone laughed nervously, anxious to please.

"But look, I gotta ask you something and I want you to be totally honest," Romeo said, stepping up to Wayne. "Just put it out there, we can take it." He paused and looked the A&R man straight in the eye. "Do you think Joe Blanchard will want to sign us?"

The question hung in the air for a moment, as all eyes fixed on Wayne.

"Shop would be lucky to have you guys," he said, shrugging. Everyone let out his breath, relieved.

Ashley giggled and made a fluttering motion with her fingers. "You hear that?" she asked. "We're going to Hollywood!" she squealed.

The band began to murmur happily, and Romeo turned to the music exec. "This is the greatest day of our lives," Ro said earnestly. "And we owe it all to you, Mr. Finebaum."

The spiky-haired man stopped smiling. "Finebaum?" he said, not understanding. "Who's Mr. Finebaum?" He looked from Hacksaw to Romeo to Myra.

Everyone spoke at once. "What?" said Romeo. "Wait, you're not —" began Myra.

The man shook his head. "I'm Miles. Miles Azoff," he said nervously.

"Miles Azoff?" repeated Louis quizzically. It took awhile to sink in.

Ashley's face fell. "Why do I feel like I'm not going to Hollywood?" she whined.

Hacksaw turned to him in confusion. "You said you were here to see The Romeo Show . . . and that you just flew in from L.A. and . . ." said Hacksaw. Hadn't he all but said he was The Shop's A&R man?

"I live in L.A.," explained Miles. "I just flew up for my brother's wedding tomorrow," he said, baffled. "Everyone told me to go to Club Scrape and check it out. . . ."

Hacksaw winced and covered his eyes. How

could he have been so incredibly stupid? He had just assumed from how the guy looked, and being from L.A. and all . . . he gave everyone a helpless look.

Romeo hung his head and looked at the ground, trying to put it together. So there had been some mix-up, and this guy *wasn't* Wild Wayne? If this guy wasn't the A&R man, then where was he?

Everyone gave murmurs of disappointment. So much for their big audition! They'd given one of their best shows ever, and no one important had been there to see it.

Myra glared at Miles. "You said you were big in the music business!" she accused him.

"Yeah," said Miles, nodding. "Assistant manager of Butch Records on La Brea," he said proudly. "Or I was. Till they went out of business," he explained with a scowl.

"But, hey," he said, his face brightening. "You guys need a roadie?"

Romeo felt sick to his stomach.

CHAPTER 4

THE GREAT ESCAPE

After sulking all night, Romeo woke up the next morning with new resolve. He'd call The Shop and invite Joe Blanchard to check the band out himself. Maybe he'd even be able to catch their act next weekend, when they had several club dates booked.

Blanchard already said he liked their music — he just needed to see what hot performers they were. Then they'd get a recording contract, no problem.

Ro gathered Gary and Louis around him in the living room and dialed The Shop. "Hey, Mr. Blanchard . . ." he began. "Wild Wayne never showed." As Joe put him on speakerphone, he pictured the busy executive getting a manicure with one hand, and signing contracts with another.

"Sorry, Romeo," said Joe. "My bad. The Kimono Twins are blowing up in Japan. They're huge. Wayne had to get there to help out," he explained.

Romeo sighed impatiently. "Look, Mr. Blanchard, forget Wild Wayne. I want to deal with you. So when can you come up to Seattle to check us out?" He heard Joe flipping the pages of his appointment book.

"Let's see," said Joe. "I'm in Los Angeles for the next two days, then New York for a day of meetings," he reported. "China for a tour, Costa Rica for some R&D," he added. "Then I really start to get busy."

The three boys looked at each other. Was this guy for real? Louis grabbed the phone from Ro. "Dude, do you ever sleep?" he asked. Ro snatched the receiver back.

"Sleep . . . sleep," said Joe, as if trying to recall what that was. "Let's try to schedule in some sleep," he called to his assistant. "Two hours, at least. Some of that REM stuff," he joked. "Look, Romeo, I can see you guys play in . . ." Romeo heard pages flipping again. "Six months," he said.

"Six months?" repeated Romeo, looking at his brothers in dismay. No way were they going to wait *six months*. Romeo punched the couch pillow angrily.

"Or you can come to Los Angeles before I leave," said Joe.

Romeo paused. "You say that's in two days?" he asked. On the other end, he heard Joe conferring with his assistant.

"Two days," said Joe. "Yep, that's right."

Romeo did some quick calculations. The drive from Seattle to L.A. was at least fifteen hours. To make it there before Joe left, they'd have to leave . . . well, *now*.

On the other hand, there was no way he was going to put his future on hold for half a year.

"Then I guess we're on our way," said Ro, lifting his chin up.

"What?!?" said Gary and Louis in unison.

"Look," Ro said into the phone, as much to his brothers as to Joe. "We're not going to let this pass us up." Ro took a deep breath, trying to sound confident. "We'll see you in L.A. in less than forty-eight hours," he said, hanging up before Joe could respond.

Louis and Gary looked at him like he was nuts.

"We're going to L.A.?" Louis said, looking dubious.

Gary was more outspoken. "You're crazy," he said, shaking his braided head in a mixture of fear and admiration.

Romeo knew he had a reputation for getting in over his head sometimes. He had to reassure Louis and Gary that this was no big deal. "We can do it, guys," he said firmly. "We have to."

But inside, his mind flooded with questions. With his parents away, Jodi was in charge — she'd never give them permission for a road trip. How would the three of them sneak out of the house without her knowing? And if they did manage to get away, how would they explain a four-day absence?

Plus, once they got on the road, they'd have to stay somewhere overnight. Would they find a motel that allowed underage guests? Romeo would have to empty his bank account to pay for gas, tolls, and lodging. The whole thing would take some planning.

Romeo bit his lip as he shot upstairs.

They had fifteen minutes to figure it out.

*   *   *

Up in their bedroom, Gary and Louis stuffed clothes into a suitcase while Ro studied a map on the computer. The three of them shared one large, comfortable bedroom, usually cluttered with posters, books, CDs, and sports equipment. Now the room was strewn with clothes and suitcases as well.

Romeo clicked on the map before him to see it in more detail. "Okay, we've got a thousand miles of driving ahead of us," he said. "Which means we should get there in . . ." he glanced at Gary, the math whiz.

"Average fifty miles per hour, stops for gas, bathroom . . ." said Gary, grabbing his calculator.

Louis poked his head out of the closet, where he was gathering sports equipment. "Don't forget food," he added. "We need to eat."

Louis was always looking forward to his next meal, especially if it involved his favorite snacks: pizza and ice cream. After this reminder, he dove back into the closet.

Gary punched numbers into his calculator. "We

should get there in exactly . . ." he added it all up. "Two days," he said.

Romeo pointed his finger at Gary. "I'm ready," he announced.

Lou emerged from the closet wearing a scuba-diving mask and flippers. Under his arm, he carried a giant red and white boogie board covered in flame decals. He tore off his flippers and threw them on top of the overflowing suitcase.

Romeo looked at his brother, decked out like a crazy surf rat. "Um, what are you doing?" he asked, pointing to his gear.

Lou set the boogie board against the bunk bed they shared. "Ro, we're going to L.A.," he pointed out. "Which means we'll be by the beach. Which reminds me, Gary . . ." He turned to his younger brother. "Factor in some aquatic activities time. . . ."

Ro jumped up from his computer. "Louis — forget aquatics!" he cried. "This is a mission," he said passionately. "We're going to L.A., getting Joe to sign us, and then coming straight back here before anyone notices that we're gone."

To make sure the game plan was clear, he went over to the suitcase and took out Louis's flippers. As Louis started to protest, Jodi walked into the room.

"What are you guys doing?" she asked suspiciously, eyeing the open suitcase and water toys. Romeo looked up at her with a false smile. "Nothing," he said, going back to his packing.

"Nothing," agreed Gary, wedging sneakers into a duffel bag.

"Going on a mission to L.A.," piped up Louis without thinking.

Ro and Gary glared at him. Louis didn't use his head sometimes! Ro gave his brother a shove, and Lou straightened up. "I mean, did I say L.A.?" chuckled Louis, removing his diving mask. "I meant, um . . ."

"Tacoma," Ro blurted, thinking quickly.

"Exactly," said Louis, nodding at Ro.

"For the . . . game," Romeo explained, his mind racing.

"What game?" asked Jodi sharply, shifting her weight.

"You know, the state . . ." Ro's eyes scanned the room and spotted the toy basketball net attached to the bunk bed. ". . . basketball finals!" He looked at Louis and Gary to back him up. Louis smiled and mimed a jump shot. Gary nodded vigorously.

Ro slapped Louis on the back, signaling it was time to end this conversation. He zipped up the suit-case and wheeled it out of the room, waving at Jodi. "You just take care of Bobby, and we'll call you from the road," he called to his older sister.

Gary grabbed his duffel and followed, putting up his hand to say good-bye, without making eye contact. Louis grabbed more bags and turned to Jodi, "*Not* the road to L.A.," he added.

As Jodi stared at him, Ro motioned to Louis from behind Jodi's back, making a "cut" gesture around his neck. He wanted to nix any more mention of their destination. In another minute, Louis would probably give her Joe Blanchard's address! He had to get them out of here.

In a flash, the boys tumbled down the stairs, leaving Jodi alone in their bedroom. "Guys!" she called after them, but she heard the front door slam. Bobby was due to wake up any minute, so she had to think fast. What were the boys up to?

She looked around their bedroom for clues to this urgent "mission." It looked as chaotic as ever, with its piles of books and toys and clothing. Then her eyes hit upon Ro's computer.

Jodi checked out the monitor. A map was still on the screen with the route from Seattle to L.A. highlighted in blue. Next to the mouse, a red and white business card caught her eye. Jodi picked it up and read it out loud. "Joe Blanchard, President, The Shop . . . Hollywood," she said. "Hollywood?" she repeated.

Ro, Lou, and Gary were going to *Hollywood?* She put the card down, shaking her head. What had the boys gotten themselves into this time? She heard Gary's car sputter and pull away from the house.

She took out her cell phone and pressed the first speed dial. Percy picked up right away. "Dad," Jodi said, cradling the phone while looking out the window. "Danger alert: the boys are thinking again. . . ."

CHAPTER 5

A STAR IS BORN

Jodi wheeled Bobby up to the waiting room of the commercial agency. For his first audition, Jodi had Bobby decked out in his cutest outfit, printed with tiny cars and trucks. What casting director could resist him?

At first, she'd refused Hacksaw's suggestion of bringing Bobby to the audition. The baby was too young, and Angeline might not approve. But then Hacksaw had persuaded her, saying it was a real opportunity. What harm could there be in trying it, just this once?

She opened the door and wheeled Bobby in. Inside, she was unprepared for the sea of babies she encountered: chubby ones, curly-haired, bald, beribboned — they seemed to come in every shape and size imaginable. There must have been fifty infants in the room, squirming and gurgling, unaware they were all competing to be the next face of Crandall's Baby Food.

Hacksaw looked out of place among the mothers and babies. "Good, you're here," he said, rising to greet them. In his ever-present sunglasses and a flashy striped shirt, he looked like he was going to a nightclub. He put down the copy of *Infant World Magazine*, which he had found on the table.

"Let me see Bobby," he demanded, bending down to face the baby.

He spoke to the baby as though he were one of his adult clients. "Okay, Bobby, this is it. Your coming-out party," he explained, pointing at him. "Now, you remember: you pay attention, you laugh at the casting director's jokes, and you smile."

Hacksaw acted out some of his instructions with hand gestures. Jodi shook her head. "Hacksaw, have you lost your mind?" she asked, throwing her hands out. "He's seven months old."

"Never too young to learn the tricks of the

trade," insisted Hacksaw. He looked at Bobby again, and pointed to his own mouth. "Smile. . . ." he commanded in a high voice. Bobby grinned up at him and pounded his stroller tray, as if demanding an ovation.

Over the loudspeaker, they heard Bobby's name announced. Hacksaw and Jodi looked at each other — time to go! Hacksaw offered his hand to Bobby, touching his tiny fist to wish him good luck. "Okay, Bobby, this is it," he said earnestly. "You do your thing."

He pulled his hand away from Bobby. It was covered in drool. Babies had even worse manners than musicians, he decided, reaching for a tissue. Jodi laughed and the two of them strolled the baby into the casting room.

Meanwhile, in the car, Ro, Gary, and Lou nodded happily to a loud rap song. They were already two hundred miles out of Seattle. With the stereo cranked up loud to their favorite tunes, the first couple hours of the ride had been a breeze. In fact, it had been a blast.

They loved cruising down the highway in Gary's red car, a hot set of wheels with yellow flame designs. Gary had won it in a radio call-in contest when he was eight, and the station had delivered it to the Miller home. Nobody had realized the winner was in second grade.

At first, Gary had been reluctant to lend out the car, wanting to keep it in top shape until he could drive it himself. But now he often shared it with his siblings, realizing they came in handy as chauffeurs.

Louis drummed on the dashboard while Ro drove. "Los Angeles, look out!" he warned.

Gary poked his head out of the backseat. "You sure we don't need to tell Dad?" he asked.

"Yeah!" Ro said, a little too emphatically. "We don't want to interrupt his vacation with Ang. Plus, he always said," — Ro deepened his voice to mimic his father. — "'If you want to make things happen, make them happen.' He'll be fine."

Lou smiled at Ro's imitation of Percy. But he was worried, too. "He will?" he asked, turning to his brother for reassurance.

"No," admitted Romeo. "But saying that makes me feel better." The truth was, Romeo knew his father wouldn't have endorsed their taking off by themselves to see Joe Blanchard. He'd have told them to be patient, and work on their act until The Shop could see them in Seattle.

On the other hand, Percy always encouraged the kids to go out and get what they wanted. As a well-known record producer, Percy could have given The Romeo Show an easy "in" to the music business. But he wanted the kids to make it on their own.

They'd come an awfully long way, but now they had the chance to go even further. On some level, Romeo suspected Percy would respect their initiative. That is, if he ever got over being furious at them for leaving without his permission.

"Know what?" said Louis. "I'm going to pretend it makes me feel better, too." He and Romeo smiled at each other.

Being part of the Miller family was the best thing that had ever happened to Louis Testaverde — or Louis Miller, as he was now known. The thought of disappointing Percy filled him with an almost physical pain. But he deferred to Ro in decisions like this — after all, he'd been a Miller longer than Lou had.

Ro turned up the stereo and cranked up another rockin' rap tune. The music drowned out their worries as they swayed to the beat, shouting lyrics at the top of their lungs.

Back at the agency, Jodi wheeled Bobby out of the casting room. She looked at the walls, lined with photos of famous actors. One day, Bobby's picture would be up there, too, she thought.

Hacksaw practically tackled Jodi from behind. "I just talked to the director," he said, catching his breath. "He LOOOOOOOOVED Bobby!" he exclaimed, delivering the news proudly.

"Of course he did, " said Jodi matter-of-factly. "'Cause Bobby's the cutest baby in the world," she cooed in a singsong voice. "No — in the universe!" she corrected herself.

Hacksaw's voice came down a notch. "Yeah, well, he didn't love him that much," he said flatly, shaking his head.

"Say what?" asked Jodi, not understanding.

Hacksaw explained that it was down to Bobby and another baby. "How could any other baby compete with Bobby?" Jodi asked, genuinely puzzled.

Just then, a stroller pulled up next to them. Jodi did a double take as she noticed the baby carriage equivalent of a Rolls Royce beside her. The seat was lined in luscious fur and black satin, and the tray was tricked out with lights, rhinestones, and silver trim.

The stroller tray even featured a sign that said, BLING BABY. Oh, brother, thought Jodi. Why not just put his name up in neon lights?

On the throne was a caramel-colored infant with wraparound shades and a killer smile. His hair was twirled into tiny clusters — the most fashionable 'do Jodi had ever seen on an infant. Bobby peered at him over his stuffed animals.

Hacksaw whispered in Jodi's ear. "That kid. His name's Mercy," he explained. "See that smile?" he said. "Pure gold."

Jodi shrugged. "He isn't cuter than Bobby," she retorted with a sassy smile.

The tall, beautiful mocha-skinned woman pushing

the carriage stopped abruptly. She peeled off her sunglasses to look at Hacksaw, Jodi, and Bobby. "Good luck, Hacksaw," she said sarcastically.

The woman then glanced down at Bobby, who smiled at her happily. "Cute kid," she sneered. "Doesn't look tough enough for this business, though," she said airily. With a toss of her long hair, she put her sunglasses back on and jerked the stroller away, floating down the hall.

Jodi's jaw dropped in amazement. "Oh, no," she said. "Tell me she didn't just diss my baby brother," Jodi said. Hacksaw looked uncomfortable. "Hacksaw, Bobby is going to get this commercial, and he's going to get it NOW."

Jodi's blood was boiling. Nobody was going to tell *her* that Bobby didn't have what it took to be on TV. She had to prove this woman wrong — no matter what it took. And when Jodi made her mind up, there was no stopping her.

With new resolve, Jodi pivoted the stroller around and headed back into the director's office. To Bobby, she said, "Now, let's go give that director a piece of our minds."

Hacksaw looked after them uneasily. Jodi was determined, but she didn't know what she was up against. Like the music biz, acting was very, very competitive. At eight months old, baby Mercy was already a pro — while Bobby was just getting started.

All Jodi knew was, Bobby was going to become the next face of Crandall's Baby Food. She thought about baby Mercy's mother, dismissing Bobby with a toss of her head.

Failure was *not* an option.

CHAPTER 6

MYSTERY MAN

On the road, Gary and Ro stretched out on the hood of Gary's car, taking a break from driving. They had stopped at a convenience store for gas and supplies. Ro took a deep breath, enjoying the sunny day.

"Know what that's the smell of?" he asked Gary dreamily.

"Air?" guessed Gary.

"Freedom, Gary," he said dramatically. "Freedom."

"Freedom smells pretty good," said Gary, inhaling the smell of grass. "So how many miles have we driven so far?" he asked.

"About three hundred and fifty," Romeo reported happily. "We should hit our halfway mark by sundown tonight," he calculated. "Which means we'll be more than halfway to the promised land by morning," he announced.

Gary laughed. "The promised land?" he said. "You mean we're going to the U.S. Mint?" Romeo looked at his little brother and smiled. Gary was a born businessman, always plotting how to make a fortune.

They heard the crackle of plastic bags behind them. "Hey, guys," said Louis, holding up several bags. "I got all four food groups." Ro and Gary climbed down off the car to examine the bounty.

"I got fruit —" said Louis, clutching a bag of sugary dried apricots. "I got grain. . . ." He waved a package of angel food snack cakes in front of them. "And I got dairy. . . ." He pulled out a bottle of chocolate milk and handed it to Gary. "Oh," Lou remembered. "And that very special taste that cannot be duplicated . . . beef jerky." He tossed Gary another package, and they started to dig in.

"Not a bad four-course meal," said Gary, tearing into the snack cakes.

"Yeah, I take my foodstuffs very seriously," said Lou in a grave voice. He wasn't happy unless the car was stuffed with three months' worth of food supplies. His greatest fear in life was reaching for a cookie and finding an empty bag.

Romeo clapped his hands together and smiled. "Okay, guys, we've chilled, we've grubbed, and even breathed in the air. . . . Now it's time to hit the road again," he coaxed. "Come on."

Gary and Lou gave groans of resistance. They'd barely had time to relax! It was nice stretching out on the hood of the car and drinking in the sunshine. In Seattle, the weather had been cool and rainy.

"Just a few more minutes," begged Louis. He was dangling a strip of beef jerky above his mouth and taking hungry bites. His idea of a gourmet meal, thought Gary.

Romeo shook his head. He was tired of being cooped up in the car, too. But they had to keep on schedule — Joe Blanchard wouldn't wait.

As they piled into the car, Gary noticed a man watching them on the other side of the parking lot. In his cowboy hat, long brown hair, and greasy goatee, he leaned against a brown van, with a sucker between his lips.

Gary realized the man had been watching them while they ate and talked. Out of the corner of his eye, he'd seen the guy's eyes follow them as they stretched out on the car, went into the convenience store, and tore into their snacks.

Probably some bored traveler, Gary figured, amused by the boys' antics. In his oversize shorts, neck chains, and b-boy cap, Romeo often attracted attention in his colorful hip-hop gear. People were always checking him out.

Gary didn't think much more about it as the car swung back on to the highway. But the brown van was following right behind them.

"L.A., here we come," shouted Romeo. "Ain't nothing gonna stop us now!" The boys whooped and hollered. Then Gary looked out the back window and saw the creepy guy from the convenience store right on their tail.

He narrowed his eyes, making sure it was the same guy. Definitely, he decided. But why was he following them?

He almost pointed him out to his brothers, but Ro and Lou were busy arguing over which CD to listen to. When Gary looked back again, another car had cut behind them. Maybe the whole thing had just been a coincidence.

Lou turned the music up again, and Gary sang along, forgetting everything except the driving beat.

A few hours later, they pulled up to a roadside motel. As he opened the door to their room, Louis gave a celebratory yell. He threw his suitcase on the floor and leaped on the bed.

"Dude, we're living like rock stars!" he shouted, jumping up and down. Gary hopped on with him, treating the bed like a trampoline. Romeo grabbed the remote and started surfing channels.

"Ro, I can't believe the clerk at the check-in desk gave you a key," marveled Lou. "No questions asked." They laughed happily. No one had dreamed it would be that easy.

Luckily, the night clerk had been practically a teenager himself. He seemed happy to give them their room key quickly, so he could go back to his comic book.

Ro pointed at Lou. "When you're shaving once a day," he said, "they'll treat *you* like an adult, too." He popped a strip of dried fruit into his mouth.

"What are you talking about?" Lou squawked, jumping off the bed. "You shave, like, once a week."

"Don't be defensive, Lou," said Gary cheerfully. "I can't shave either," he said as he bounced on the bed. "Although it feels like something is growing . . . right there." Gary leaped off the bed abruptly and pointed to his chin.

Romeo bent down to examine him. "No, I don't see anything," he reported apologetically. He scanned his brother's smooth skin with his fingers.

"Trust me," said Gary. "It'll be there. A-a-any day now," he predicted. He couldn't wait to be a teenager, drive his car, and start making some *real* money. Lou and Ro laughed at Gary's impatience to grow up. As it was, he was like a thirty-year-old in a ten-year-old's body.

Lou dug into his bag and pulled out three bottles of water, tossing them backhand to Ro and Gary. "A toast, guys," he said, holding up the plastic bottle like it was champagne. "To our first road trip," he said. "And to having clean underwear."

They all laughed and clinked bottles. Lou took a hearty swig of water, then spit it out with a gasp. "Uggghhh!" he cried. "This water's about a thousand degrees."

Gary volunteered to get some ice. He stepped outside the room, enjoying the cool evening air. As he walked toward the ice machine, he saw a hulking figure perched next to a van.

In the dusk, it was hard to see. But as Gary got closer, he saw a familiar black cowboy hat and goateed face, sucking on a toothpick. It was the creepy guy!

"Arghhhhhh!" Gary screamed loudly. His braids shook as he ran back to the room.

Ro and Lou looked up as Gary rushed in and slammed the door behind him. He bolted each lock, throwing his body against the door. He was shaking. "What's wrong?" asked Romeo, walking over to Gary.

His brother started talking a mile a minute. "This sketched-out creepy guy!" he said, gasping for air. "I saw him following us in the car. Now he's outside our room." Lou and Ro looked at each other.

"He was following us in our car?" said Lou, his voice rising. "Why didn't you say anything?" he shouted.

Gary clutched Lou with both arms. "I'm saying something now!" he yelled. Ro shook his head in disbelief. They'd been in the car for hours together — why hadn't he told them?

Suddenly the TV started to flicker, and then it shut down completely. The lights in the room went out, and then came back on again. "Oh, no," moaned Lou. "This is where it starts."

"Lou," Ro warned. "Don't encourage him."

Louis grabbed Romeo's shoulders. "Ro, haven't you ever seen a horror movie?" he demanded. "First, everyone is having fun doing what they're *not* supposed to do. . . ."

"Like going on a road trip," Gary pointed out.

"Exactly!" said Lou, spinning around and pointing

at Gary. "Then someone spots some creepy guy out-side. . . ." Lou motioned dramatically. Romeo rolled his eyes.

"Then the TV goes out," added Gary, pointing at the dark screen.

Enough hysteria, thought Ro. It was time to put the brakes on. Lou and Gary were getting totally whipped up, on the basis of . . . what? "Lou, Gary," he began, sitting down on the bed. "You guys are ridiculous."

"Look!" screamed Gary.

Moving outside the window was a silhouetted figure. The boys approached cautiously, moving across the room in small steps. Ro drew back the curtains sharply, and the creepy guy was right there.

"Arrrghhhhhh!" they screamed, and the stalker looked startled, too. Romeo reached over and yanked the cord to pull the drapes.

Still shaking, they dropped on to the bed and huddled together. The doorknob started jiggling furi-ously — now the guy was trying to get into their room! Ro buried his head in his hands. This whole trip had been a disaster.

The boys were trapped. Thanks to their own cleverness, not a single person in the world knew their whereabouts. Someone was out to get them — someone motivated enough to follow them for hours across hundreds of miles. What did this guy want?

There was no way they were going outside to find out.

CHAPTER 7

CREEP SHOW

The next morning in the motel room, sunlight poured through the edges of the window. All three boys had fallen asleep sitting up and fully dressed. They were frozen in defensive positions: Lou with a plunger, Ro with a hanger, Gary clutching a pillow.

In his slumber, Lou dropped the plunger and it crashed to the floor.

Everyone jolted awake. "What?" yelled Romeo. "Who's there? Back off, man, back off!"

He sprang into action and started brandishing his hanger like it was a sword. Barely awake, he thrashed around, fending off an imaginary enemy.

"Help!" Gary screamed, burying his head in the pillow. Lou hit the floor with a loud thump.

After a few seconds of hysterics, they looked at the window, and then at each other. What were they doing?

They had spent the night cowering together on one of the double beds, panicking at the sound of every footstep. In their heightened state of fear, they trembled at every shadow at the window, and at each rush of wind through the door.

In fact, they'd been too scared to leave the room for dinner. "You think I'm going to go outside and risk running into that maniac?" Romeo had said. They had to make do with the last of their dried fruit strips and snack cakes. Lou had *not* been a happy camper.

They hadn't had many options. Calling the police was risky — they would probably have escorted the boys back to Seattle. If they'd phoned their dad, he would have discovered what they were up to, and then: Good-bye, Joe Blanchard.

Now Louis peeled himself off the floor, rubbing his backside. "Ouch, that hurt," he said.

Romeo looked at his brother. "You guys okay?" he asked.

"I'm still here," said Gary, looking down at himself for confirmation.

"We're alive!" shouted Louis. "Alive, I say!" Romeo turned to him, annoyed. It was time for everyone to take a deep breath, and chill.

"Louis, get a hold of yourself," he ordered. "Let me just do a little check."

Still carrying the hanger in front of him, Romeo headed toward the door cautiously. Lou and Gary followed close behind to provide cover. Poised with a plunger, Lou trailed after Gary, who wielded a couch pillow.

When Romeo opened the door, he blinked in the bright sunlight. He looked to the left, and then to the right. Nothing.

Romeo went back inside the room and looked at Lou and Gary. "It's all clear," said Romeo, and Louis gasped with relief. He shook his head and tossed the plunger on the bed. Gary threw his pillow down and reached for his suitcase.

Ro looked at his watch. They'd lost time this morning that they'd have to make up on the road. Plus, they were starving from having skipped a meal last night. If they didn't hustle, they wouldn't make it there in time to see Joe.

"Louis, Gary, grab your stuff and get your butts in the car," demanded Ro. "We've wasted enough timing worrying about this guy. There's nobody out there. In ten seconds, I want you in your seats, cranking a CD in the stereo."

It was time to get this show on the road.

That morning, Jodi was up early, too. She'd gotten Bobby dressed in adorable red overalls. His socks had tiny pom-poms on them, and his shoes were mini high-top sneakers. It was his big day, and Jodi wanted him to look his best.

She and Ashley wheeled Bobby into the commercial studio, and Ashley brushed back her long, black hair. "When I said I'd do you a solid, I didn't mean at six in the morning," said Ashley, pushing Bobby's stroller. She was definitely *not* a morning person.

"I know," said Jodi sympathetically. "Thanks for being here. I just want to make sure everything goes perfectly." She was a little nervous about Bobby's acting debut. What if he went into one of his crying spells?

Hacksaw came running up to them. "There's my superstar!" he thundered, pointing at Bobby. "Jodi, I've got to tell you, I don't know what you said to the director yesterday," he whispered, "but he's all aboard the Bobby train."

Jodi smiled. "I just told 'em if he hired somebody over my baby brother, he'd have to deal with my dad," she explained with a wink.

"Ah," said Hacksaw. Though he knew she was joking, he could see how Jodi would have made a strong impression. She'd probably intimidated the director. Hacksaw was a little cowed by her himself.

Just then, a tall, beautiful woman in wraparound sunglasses passed by, carrying a baby. It was baby Mercy's mother, Jodi realized. She almost didn't recognize her without her deluxe, ridiculous stroller.

"You?" she said, glaring at Jodi.

"You?" said Jodi, glaring back. They were both still steaming from their heated encounter the day before.

The woman gave a snort of disgust. "I can't believe this," she fumed. "I'm working with the baby that won out over my beautiful son?" she cried.

Then it hit Jodi: this woman was the actress who'd be playing Bobby's mother in the commercial! The woman had auditioned her own son, Mercy, for the part — but he'd lost out to Bobby. Victory felt sweet.

Jodi smiled wickedly. "Yeah, it's a tough business, isn't it?" she asked, throwing her own words back at her. The woman tossed her long, curly hair and walked away in a huff.

Finally, it was show time. The director motioned for Jodi and Ashley to go onstage and put Bobby into his high chair. As soon as he was strapped in, he began to wail uncontrollably. Jodi smiled nervously, hoping the mood would pass.

But the crying continued. Now his little body was shaking with big, heaving sobs. Jodi walked over to him and rocked him gently, hoping to calm him down. When the tears subsided, she put Bobby back in his seat.

For a moment, he was silent, and then the waterworks started up again. The actress playing his mother rolled her eyes as if to say "See? You should have chosen *my* baby. *He'd* never behave like this!"

Jodi was frantic. Didn't Bobby realize this was his big debut? She tried waving his rattle, plastic keys, and fuzzy toys. No reaction.

Why, oh, why had he chosen *this* moment to have a meltdown?

The entire stage crew hovered over Bobby in a circle, making funny faces at him. Bobby just looked at them and continued crying.

"You don't want to go back to your trailer, Bobby," begged the director. He was a theatrical man with coppery hair, a red beret, and a wildly patterned paisley shirt. He tried growling at him, clucking at him, whistling at him. Nothing worked.

Ashley covered her face with her hands and removed some of her fingers. "Peek-a-boo!" she cried.

Bobby looked up and smiled.

The crew looked at each other. "Good, Bobby," murmured Hacksaw. "That's a boy," he coached him.

He'd been sweating bullets, watching Bobby cry. Every minute that the shoot was delayed cost the company money.

The director placed Ashley in a spot directly across from Bobby, to work her magic. Now Bobby was really smiling.

"And . . . action!" said the director, with relief.

The actress brought a spoon up to Bobby's face, trying to coax his mouth open. "Bobby . . . that's a good Bobby," the director said in a low voice. Ashley made the peek-a-boo face again. Bobby looked up again and . . .

SPLAT! Bobby had flung the food onto Ashley. Her face, hair, and clothes were dripping with orange mush. She gasped loudly. Wiping the food from her eyes, she looked down at her shirt.

Oh, no! Her new sky blue, rhinestone-studded tank top was splattered with strained carrots. The top half of her body was coated with lumpy orange goo. Yuck.

Jodi smiled and shook her head sympathetically. That's what babies were like! Ashley should have known better than to wear her new top.

*   *   *

Later on the set, the director in the red beret slapped Hacksaw on the shoulder. "We made magic today," he said, handing Hacksaw a check from his shirt pocket.

Hacksaw accepted the money with pleasure. "So Bobby worked out pretty well for you?" he asked. The director nodded. Once they'd gotten past the crying spell, Bobby had been great, he said.

"I look forward to working with him again," said the director. "Maybe sooner than you think . . ."

Hacksaw pondered this comment, while the red beret turned and walked down the hall. He waited until the director was out of sight before rushing up to Jodi and shouting, "We nailed it!"

Jodi whooped with joy. They examined the check together, marveling at the amount. For three hours' work, it was impressive.

"That's a lot of zeros," said Jodi, her eyes widening. It was more than she'd ever received for a Romeo gig!

"That's what they pay you for the getting the

62

job done," said Hacksaw. Jodi smiled again, swelling with pride. Turning to Ashley, she said, "Can you get me a coffee?"

Ashley came up to them wearing a baby food stained T-shirt. A lump of orange goo was clinging to her forehead. "Uh, maybe in a sec," she said, sounding annoyed. "First, do you have an extra shirt I can borrow?"

Jodi shook her head impatiently. "Getting your hands dirty is part of the job, Ash," she said. In the past few days with Bobby, she'd gone through about ten outfits. He'd spit up on sweaters, T-shirts, jeans . . . everything.

"But is getting my shirt dirty part of it?" asked Ashley, stung by Jodi's indifference. After all, she'd gone out of her way to do her a favor — at six in the morning, yet!

"Why must you be so difficult?" said Jodi, in a patronizing tone.

Ashley threw her hands up in frustration. "But all I'm asking for is a clean shirt!" she cried.

"Whatever," Jodi sniffed. "I can't take this attitude. You're fired."

"You're not even paying me!" said Ashley, furious.

For a moment, Jodi was thrown off, realizing Ashley was right. "Well," she said, trying to recover her dignity. "You're still fired!"

Ashley's jaw dropped and Hacksaw's blue eyes opened wide. He and Ashley stared at her in disbelief. Jodi's behavior was outrageous.

Hacksaw knew that show biz could sometimes bring out the worst in people. Not everyone could handle the power, money, and attention that came with success. He'd seen musicians change overnight when they had their first hit record.

But still . . . it was hard to believe show biz had affected Jodi. She had a pretty level head on her shoulders, and Hacksaw had a lot of respect for her competence and judgment.

So why was she acting like a diva stage mom?

CHAPTER 8

ON THE ROAD

Back on the road, the boys cruised along the interstate. Romeo drove, while Louis studied the map. "Alright, Louis," said Romeo. "How much farther?"

"Only three hundred ten miles to go, man," Louis announced happily.

"Nice," agreed Romeo. "We should get there by this afternoon." Louis nodded. "Joe Blanchard," warned Romeo, "get ready to meet your next biggest band. . . ." They cranked up the tunes again and sped off.

Behind them, the man in the brown van was watching every move.

The boys kept driving. In the car, they listened to music, singing loudly to their favorite tunes. When they got tired of their CDs, they tried the radio. They surfed between rap, country, vintage rock-and-roll, and gospel. They even tried a call-in talk show.

Gary suggested they count red cars for a while. Finally they just drove along silently, each of them lost in their own thoughts.

Romeo turned to Louis, in the seat beside him. "What are you going to do when we get our first platinum record?" They loved to fantasize about future fame and fortune.

"Pizza," said Lou, without missing a beat.

"Pizza?" said Romeo quizzically.

"Yeah. Pizza," said Lou. "Dirty Thirties Pizza Palace. I'm going to sit down and have a slice of each and every kind," he said, closing his eyes. They were known for exotic pizza toppings like pineapple, anchovies, and marshmallows.

"Thirty slices of pizza?!" cried Gary. "Man, I do not want to be around when you hurl." They all laughed, picturing Lou heaving. He had a history of biting off more than he could chew — literally.

"Don't worry, I'll give you a five-second warning," Lou promised. He looked at Gary. "What are you going to do?"

"Tanning booths," replied Gary.

"Pizza's a much better call," said Lou.

Gary shook his head. "Nope," he said. "I'm going to start a chain of tanning booths. Gary's Good Looks Tanning Salons," he said. "Our motto is 'Bake It So You Can Shake It,'" he said.

Romeo laughed at his brothers. "Man, you guys have some wild imaginations," he said, adjusting his red and white baseball cap. Lou asked Ro what *he'd* do when they went platinum.

"Man, I'll just be grateful that people like our music," he said. "I'll head back into the studio and record some more."

Lou and Gary looked at each other. "What fun is that?" asked Gary. He had thought Ro would want to put in his own private basketball court, or buy a hot car.

"Yeah, Ro," added Lou. "You do that whether you go platinum or not."

"I guess I do," mused Romeo. "But what's better than having people love what you do, what you create?" Ro asked passionately. "Man, that's worth everything." He felt inspired just thinking about it.

Lou looked at him and shrugged. "I'd still rather eat pizza," he said cheerfully, and they all cracked up.

Then Romeo looked in the rearview mirror, and almost lost it. The brown van was back, right on their tail. They had been driving for hours. This guy was clearly after them.

Back at the commercial agency, Myra pushed Bobby's stroller, enjoying the bustle of the busy corridors.

She was a smart, fun-loving sixteen-year-old, and she liked being around the lively Miller clan. When the agency had asked Bobby to star in another commercial, Myra was glad to lend a hand.

"Thanks for helping," said Jodi, turning to Myra. "I really appreciate it." Hacksaw gave her arm a squeeze to show he was grateful, too. After Ashley had stormed out, Jodi had been lucky to line up another helper.

"No problem," said Myra sincerely. She looked around, wondering if she'd spot any famous actors.

"I had some problems with my last assistant,"

Jodi explained. She was still annoyed at Ashley, freaking out over a stained shirt.

Myra looked at the wall lined with head shots. "Don't worry, Jodi," Myra reassured her. "I'm here to help." Myra and Jodi looked at each other and smiled.

As she entered the stage area, Jodi's face darkened. "A blue background?" she said, turning to Hacksaw. "I hate blue, Hacksaw," she said.

Hacksaw yelled, "Change the background, people!" He wasn't sure how the director would feel about Jodi giving orders. Dozens of babies were on stage, surrounded by colorful building blocks. Above them was a logo for the toy company.

Jodi climbed on to the stage and picked up a small plastic toy. "This isn't going to work," she announced angrily. "Bobby could swallow this piece and choke."

She handed the piece to Hacksaw, and he handed it to Myra. "You, take this far away," he instructed her. "In fact, bury it." Myra took the plastic toy and stuffed it into her pocket.

Jodi motioned for Myra to join her onstage. "Bring Bobby on," she ordered.

Myra bristled at her tone. "Um, a 'please' would be nice," she told Jodi, who repeated the command.

"Please," Jodie added, in a bored tone.

Myra sighed and lifted Bobby out of this stroller. A man in a red beret and wildly patterned shirt entered the stage. Jodi recognized him as the director, the same man who had directed Bobby in the baby food commercial.

With a raised hand, he signaled it was time to begin. "Now I, Maurice Maurice, will make baby magic," he announced. He pointed at center stage. "The baby goes here," he said.

"Um," said Jodi. "Excuse me, Mr. Director, but I think the light is much better over here." She pointed to a corner of the stage. "Bobby needs to look his best."

. The director was taken aback. "And you are?" he asked, approaching Jodi with raised eyebrows.

"Jodi Miller," she said proudly. "The star's guardian. We've met," she said, extending her hand to shake.

He kissed it instead. "Right," he said smoothly. "I'm not too good with faces. Or names." He shouted to someone off stage. "The baby stays here."

"Uh, no, he doesn't," explained Jodi. "He does what I say or he goes home." She turned to Myra. "Move Bobby over here," she ordered.

The director stalked off the set, and said to his assistant, "Get me a producer."

"Move Bobby over here, 'please,'" corrected Myra.

Jodi waved her away impatiently. "Myra, I don't have time for this," she said, throwing up her hands. "Hacksaw, take the baby. Myra . . . you're fired," said Jodi.

"What?" Myra gasped. "Why?"

"Because you're irritating me," Jodi said, tossing her head. "Plus," she confided with a giggle, "I'm starting to like this whole firing thing."

Myra stared at her, flabbergasted. She'd rearranged her schedule to help Jodi out, and *this* was the thanks she got? She grabbed her jacket and walked out, shaking with anger. Leaving the stage area, she nearly tripped on a colorful plastic building block.

She tossed it into the nearest garbage can.

At the spa, Angeline relaxed in the steam room, stretching out luxuriously in her bikini top and colorful sarong. Percy opened the door, wearing his fluffy white bathrobe.

"Hey, honey," she said, puzzled. "Why are you wearing a robe in the steam room?" It was at least ninety degrees in there. Percy pulled his robe belt tighter. "There are a lot of strangers walking around," he said suspiciously, peering through the glass door. He didn't feel like parading around in his bathing suit.

"It's just me," insisted Angeline. "Okay, baby, I've had enough." She stood up and patted him on the shoulder. "I'm going to go back up to the room."

"I'll just sit here and meditate," he said, giving her a kiss. Angeline looked at him with concern.

"Alright," she said. "Don't stay too long." She knew it was easy to lose track of time in the steam room.

Staying longer than the twenty-minute time limit was a bad idea, she warned. Too much exposure to the high temperature could be dangerous.

Percy nodded in agreement. He had visited the steam room only to please Angeline — there was no danger of him staying too long. But as he laid his head against the moist tiles, he found the heat relaxing.

Just for a few moments, he told himself.

Then his eyes began to close.

As Angeline closed the door, she slipped on her bathrobe, which was hanging on a hook nearby. As she pulled the robe on, she knocked over a janitor's mop leaning against the wall.

Percy looked up just in time to see the mop catch on the door handle, trapping him in the steam room.

CHAPTER 9

TRAPPED!

Percy got up and pounded on the door. "Ang . . . ANG!" he shouted at the top of his lungs. But she had already left. Looking through the glass, he saw the room outside was completely empty.

He pounded again, but it was useless. The place was deserted. If only he had brought his cell phone! But Angie had urged him to leave it behind and enjoy the spa's restful atmosphere.

Well, there was nothing restful about getting locked in the steam room. Percy sat down on the wooden bench and mopped his brow. Now he was *really* sweating.

He buried his head in his hands, realizing his fate.

* * *

Deep in the middle of nowhere, Gary's car came to a screeching halt. "L.A. is two hundred miles away?!" Romeo shouted. He couldn't believe his ears. Louis frantically looked through the maps spread out on his lap.

They had stopped the car in front of a red barn and could barely hear themselves over the sound of mooing cows. "Louis," said Romeo, trying to keep his cool. "How are we farther from L.A. than we were THREE HOURS AGO?"

Ro looked around unhappily at the country road they were on, surrounded by green fields and tractors. *Not* exactly Sunset Boulevard.

"Good question," put in Gary. He was playing a video game in the backseat.

Louis studied one of the maps, trying to puzzle it out. "We got on the five outside of San Francisco, traveled down the seven-ten, and then . . . uh," he said, looking at them helplessly. "I have no idea, guys."

"What a surprise," said Gary, shaking his head. Lou had been more focused on trying to find the right radio station.

Ro turned to him, deadly serious. "Louis, Joe

Blanchard is going to be out of our lives in twelve hours," he said. "And so will our chance to be able to do business with him." Didn't Lou know how important this was?

Gary turned around in the backseat and saw the brown van parked right behind them. "Romeo . . ." he said. He could see the guy's black cowboy hat through the windshield.

But Ro and Lou were arguing over the map. "So where are we exactly?" Ro asked.

Louis turned the map around and pointed to a spot. "I think here . . . or maybe here," he guessed.

"Romeo . . ." repeated Gary, his voice growing more desperate.

His brothers continued to bicker. "You're the navigator," Romeo said to Lou. "You're always sup- posed to navigate." He snatched the map out of Lou's hands. "Give me that!" he said.

"ROMEO!!" Gary yelled, clutching at Romeo's jacket.

"What?" shouted Romeo, turning to face the backseat. Couldn't Gary see he was trying to get them out of this mess?

Gary pointed out the back window and showed Lou and Ro the brown van. The creepy guy in the cowboy hat honked his horn and saluted.

"That's the man who's been following us," screamed Gary.

"Ro, come on, let's go," Louis shouted. Ro rubbed his hands and thought for a moment.

"Yeah, Ro, let's get out here," pleaded Gary.

Lou was frantic now. "No kidding. He's been following us since Seattle."

Gary spoke rapidly. "He's probably some road maniac that wants to rob us, steal my car, and leave us here to rot and get eaten by vultures!" Romeo rolled his eyes.

Suddenly, they heard the van door slam behind them, and the scrape of the man's boots on the asphalt.

"Exactly what I was thinking," said Louis. "Come on, Ro. Let's go. Let's get out of here."

Lou and Gary watched in terror as the man approached the car. Ro put the map down. "Louis, I'm not running," he said. "Nothing's going to stop us getting to Joe."

Abruptly, Romeo jumped out of the car. It was time to face the enemy. The creepy guy was walking toward them.

"Hey, man," Romeo said, pointing to the stranger. "You better back off."

The guy smiled and kept moving. Romeo could get a better look at him now. A sucker dangled from his lips. He wore a black cowboy hat and had long hair and a goatee. He looked like a lowlife drifter — or maybe a country singer.

"You think this is funny?" Ro continued. "You're about to get a rain of pain." With this threat, he began slashing the air in a series of mad karate chops. "Aaaaaaiiiii-yah!" he screamed, thrashing wildly.

A guy passing by in a tractor turned his neck to watch Romeo's grunts and kicks. Ro's diamond ear-ring studs and hip-hop gear made him look out of place next to a hog pen.

"Come on," Romeo begged, taunting the stranger to attack.

Gary and Louis got out of the car and stood next to Ro. The man seemed unfazed by Romeo's bogus martial arts moves. Without removing the sucker from between his lips, he drawled, "Seems like you're lost."

"We *are* lost," Louis blurted. "It doesn't just seem like it."

"Louis, stop talking," instructed Gary.

Romeo pointed at the man. "You've been following us," he accused him.

The man held up his hands and smiled. "Guilty as charged," he said.

"What's your deal, man?" asked Romeo.

"My deal . . . ?" the man asked, reaching into his jacket. The boys shrank back in fear, expecting him to pull out a gun.

Instead, he handed them a business card. "You boys need to relax, man," he said. Romeo took the card.

"'Andrew Fisher, Director of Creative Issues, Percy Miller Records,'" he read. Louis and Gary gasped. Good grief!

"You work for our dad?" Ro asked in disbelief. This was *too* weird.

"Yup," he said, pulling a caramel-colored sucker

out of his mouth. "Your sister, Jodi, told your dad that you were going on this little road trip," he said. "So he wanted me to keep an eye on you."

Ro and Louis looked at each other, deflated.

"Which seems like a good idea since you've been driving in circles for about four hours," Andrew pointed out.

"I can explain that —" Louis began defensively.

"So," said Ro, trying to absorb the situation. "Our dad knows we're on a road trip?" he asked. Andrew nodded. Romeo shook his head, imagining his dad's anger when he heard the news.

"I wish you *were* the road maniac," admitted Gary. "That would be less scary than Dad knowing what we're doing." Lou and Romeo agreed.

Andrew laughed in sympathy. "Yeah, your dad can be kind of tough," he confided. Then he quickly reassured them. "Not that I don't love working for him. In fact, make sure you tell your dad how I said he's the best boss in the world," he said.

"But you didn't say that," Lou pointed out.

"Your dad is the best boss in the whole world," he said.

"Okay, I'll tell him," said Lou grudgingly.

"Cool," said Andrew. Romeo and Lou looked at each other. They still couldn't believe their stalker worked for their dad.

"Anyway," Andrew continued, "I know where you're going, so just follow me and we'll get you to Joe Blanchard's office." He motioned for them to follow his van.

The boys perked up at this news. "Cool," they said at the same time, breaking into smiles. Finally, things were looking up.

The only trouble was, they were almost out of time. Joe would be leaving his office shortly, and they were hundreds of miles away.

Ro shot a grateful glance at Andrew. Suddenly, he was their only hope.

CHAPTER 10

NO ADMITTANCE

As they pulled into Los Angeles, the boys were dazzled by the sights they saw: wild punk rockers with pink Mohawks, palm trees in Beverly Hills, huge billboards on the Sunset Strip. Seattle seemed tiny and sleepy by comparison.

They followed Andrew's van to a shimmering glass tower in the downtown business district. Somewhere in this skyscraper was Joe Blanchard, if he hadn't left town already. The boys looked up at the fifty-story building.

"Wow, we really made it," marveled Romeo, pulling up to the building. "Come on," he said. They tumbled out of the car, and Andrew met them on the steps of the building.

"Andrew, watch the car," Gary ordered.

Andrew frowned, noticing it was in a no-parking zone. Gary remembered how only a few hours earlier, they'd been deathly scared of Andrew. Actually, he'd turned out to be a handy guy to have around.

The boys went through the revolving door, gazing up at the immense marble and glass lobby. They approached the security desk, and a hip young blond woman met their eyes. She wore a short orange jacket and had fashionably tousled hair.

"I'm here to see Joe Blanchard," announced Romeo eagerly. The woman's eyes moved over the three of them, taking in their age and sloppy appearance.

"Name?" she asked, raising her eyebrows.

"Romeo Miller," he replied. She checked her computer screen. Behind her, a tall, bald security guard locked eyes with Gary.

"That name is not here," she said curtly.

Romeo tried again. "The Romeo Show?" he guessed. The lady scanned her computer screen once more. Gary folded his arms and the security guard folded *his* arms.

"No, Mr. Show," she said smugly. "That name is not appearing either. Sorry."

"Try 'Louis Miller'," said Lou, stepping up to the desk. Ro and Gary gave him a look. "What?" he said with a shrug. "It was worth a shot."

Gary unfolded his arms and the guard did the same.

"Ma'am," pleaded Romeo. "Mr. Blanchard's expecting us." He gave her a broad smile. "Just holler up at him and let him know I'm here," he said.

"Yeah," echoed Lou. "Just holler."

The lady gave a short laugh. "Just 'holler'?" she repeated sarcastically. "I don't think so. Mr. Blanchard is not going to meet with some kids," she said indignantly. "He's a very busy man!"

Louis and Ro looked at each other. They had thought *getting* to Joe's building would be the hard part, not the trip up the elevator. What now?

Romeo tried to explain. "No, I talked to him," he told the receptionist. "He wants us here."

"Yeah," said Louis, backing him up. "We're a band he wants to check out."

The woman turned to the security guard, who was now in a serious stare-off with Gary. "Do they look like a band to you?" she asked.

The guard's eyes broke away from Gary reluctantly, and he shook his head no.

"Me, neither," she said cheerfully. "Escort them out."

The security guard moved in on them, his eyes still fixed on Gary. Arguing was useless, Ro realized. He put an arm on Gary's shoulder and steered toward the revolving doors. Near the exit, Lou whispered, "Don't worry. I've got an idea."

As the guard ushered them out the door, Romeo hoped Lou's idea was a good one.

An hour later, Romeo, Lou, and Gary reentered the bulding. This time, they were decked out in rock-star gear: long fur coats, shades, cowboy hats, and wigs. Romeo chatted on his cell. "Joey B., yeah, it's me, babe," he said.

The lady receptionist and the security guard eyeballed the approaching trio. "How you livin'?" Romeo said into the phone.

Louis nodded. "Ask big Joe how's he living."

"He just did," said Gary, twirling a feather boa.

"Alright," said Lou.

Gary looked up at the security guard. "What's happening?" he asked.

Ro kept talking into his cell. "Yeah, I'm here. Coming up right now . . ." he said.

Looking around, Louis asked the lady, "Where are the elevators?" He held his breath while she paused.

"Right down the hall to the left. By the way," she added, "I love your music."

"Thanks," said Romeo, blowing her a kiss.

As they turned into the elevator bank, the three of them collapsed in laughter. "I can't believe that worked!" exclaimed Lou. Ro nodded happily — usually Lou's solutions turned out to be worse than the problem.

They piled into the elevator, laughing and joking. Nothing could stop them now.

Back at the Millers', Hacksaw taped one of Bobby's head shots on to the refrigerator. Myra and Ashley leaned against the kitchen counter.

"Look, I owe you both an apology," said Jodi.

Ashley and Myra looked at each other.

"You don't say," Myra said in a bored voice.

"Really?" Ashley asked, sarcastic.

Jodi seemed not to notice. "Now that this whole Bobby thing has taken off," she confided, "we need to be around people we can trust."

"Uh-huh," said Ashley and Myra at the same time. Each of them wore an expression that said, "And *why* should I care?"

"So what do you think?" asked Jodi excitedly. "You guys can be my junior talent managers," she announced proudly.

Ashley and Myra looked at each other and shook their heads.

"Nah," said Ashley.

"I don't think so," said Myra.

Jodi accepted these answers with a nod. Then she pulled out two fifty-dollar bills and waved them in front of the girls. "Would these change your minds?" she asked.

Myra plucked one of the bills out of her hand. "It's a start," she said, lifting her chin up. She looked over at Ashley and smiled.

"A good start," agreed Ashley, taking the other bill. The three of them giggled.

"Good," said Jodi. "Now, here's a list of producers and talent agencies looking for babies." She handed them each a sheet of paper. "Start calling 'em up and selling Bobby."

"How?" asked Ashley. She had never been a salesperson.

Hacksaw walked by, talking on his cell. "That's right," he said. "He's hot off of two commercials. If you don't snap him up now, you're going to lose out on a hu-u-u-uge cash cow." He gave the girls a wink. "And your producer will fire you," he added.

"Like that," said Jodi, pointing to Hacksaw.

The phone rang and Jodi pounced on it. "Hello, Miller Talent Agency," she said, trying to sound brisk and professional.

"Jodi?" asked a puzzled voice. It was Angeline.

Jodi's eyes widened. "Uh, hey, Ang, I was hoping it was you," she lied, trying to think fast. "You guys having fun?"

"Um, yeah," said Angeline. "How's the baby?"

"Great," said Jodi in a falsely bright voice. "He's great."

Angeline paused a moment. "What's the Miller Talent Agency?" she asked.

Jodi cringed, looking around the kitchen transformed by giant publicity photos. "Well . . . you see," she laughed nervously, stalling for time.

But before she had to come up with an answer, she heard her dad's voice in the background. He was asking for water, but his voice sounded strange.

"Jodi, I'll talk to you later,"Angeline said before hanging up quickly.

Saved for the moment! thought Jodi. Luckily, her parents wouldn't be home for a few more days. She'd figure out how to deal with them then.

In the meantime, they'd have to work fast. She motioned for Myra and Ashley to get cracking.

CHAPTER 11

SAY IT AIN'T SO, JOE

On the thirty-second floor of an L.A. office building, Louis, Ro, and Gary poured out of the elevator, laughing and high-fiving. Looking down at their rock-star garb, they still couldn't believe they'd pulled it off. This time, Ro had to hand it to Lou.

"Good plan, bro," he said, slapping Louis on the back.

"I've got some good ideas," said Louis. "What can I say?"

"Unfortunately, you've got more bad ideas," said Gary, adjusting an enormous wig sprouting dreadlocks.

"What?" asked Lou. His plan was brilliant. Luckily, Andrew had known some secondhand shops on Melrose that had just the right blend of grunge and glamour.

"I'm gonna hit the john," said Louis.

"Me, too," said Gary. "I've got to get out of these leopard pants," he complained. "They're itchy."

"Cool," said Ro. "Get rid of this while you're at it. He took off his black leather motorcycle jacket and handed it to Gary.

"Uhhhh," Louis pointed to Ro's head to remind him he was still in costume.

"Right," said Ro, removing his wild, spike-haired wig.

Gary and Louis hit the bathroom while Romeo leaned against a marble wall and took in the scenery. A couple of punk rockers walked by. A tall, beautiful girl with sandy hair smiled at him. A guy in a silver jacket and sunglasses chatted on his cell.

Turning the corner was a good-looking, dark-skinned man with a shaved head. He was trim and fit, in a striped blue and white shirt with a gold chain around his neck. Romeo realized who it was.

"Mr. Blanchard!" he said putting out his hand. Up close, Romeo noticed he had two diamond stud earrings in one ear. Around his neck, he wore a wire-less mouthpiece.

Joe gave his palm a squeeze. "Romeo!" he said with surprise. "You actually made it."

"Said I would," said Romeo, as though two days of traveling were no big deal. "Where do you want us to set up?"

Joe laughed. "How about the Greek Theater?"

Romeo's jaw dropped. "What?" he squeaked.

"Today's your lucky day, son. My opening act just canceled on JoJo," explained Joe. "The spot's yours if you want it. If you do well, The Shop will sign you to a record deal and put you on tour."

Opening for JoJo? At the Greek Theater? Romeo was floored.

"Mr. Blanchard," he said. "That's amazing. We'll be ready." Where were Louis and Gary? They were going to be blown away.

"Hey, whoa, Romeo," Blanchard stopped him. "There is no 'we.' The show only has room for a solo artist," Joe explained.

"But," Romeo sputtered, "I do all my songs with my band. They're my family —"

Joe cut him off. "Look, Ro, that's sweet," he said. "Really. But I only need a rapper — no one else.

If you can't do it, I'll get someone else." He shrugged matter-of-factly. "Let me know, okay?"

He turned down the hall and disappeared behind smoked-glass doors. Just then, Louis and Gary burst out of the bathroom.

Romeo was crushed. Joe Blanchard had just offered him the biggest break of his career, opening for a major pop star. The Greek Theater was a famed rock arena — just about every music star in the world had performed there. How could he turn that down?

Ro had never felt more miserable. Either he could turn down the chance of a lifetime or turn his back on his family. Some choice!

But when he saw Gary and Louis coming back from the bathroom, he knew he couldn't do it. They'd be devastated if they were left out, especially after all they'd gone through to get here. He couldn't imagine telling them that he was breaking into the big leagues — without them.

Before they could speak, Ro brought up his hand to silence them. "Come on, guys," he said. "We're going home."

*   *   *

Romeo, Lou, and Gary let the revolving doors spin behind them. It took a moment for their eyes to adjust to the blinding sunshine.

Heading back to the car, Louis and Gary were totally confused. In the five minutes they'd been apart, Ro decided he wanted to go home and skip their audition for Joe Blanchard. What happened?

"Uh, Romeo," said Louis, trying again. "We just traveled a thousand miles to audition for the man and we're leaving after 'hello'?" He threw up his hands in frustration.

"Well, what'd Joe say?" asked Gary, mystified by Ro's sudden turnaround.

Romeo shrugged impatiently. "Nothing, Gary," he said. "It's just not gonna happen, okay?" He wished they'd just drop the subject.

When they came back to the car, Andrew was leaning against it. He jumped up when he saw them, removing the sucker from his mouth. "How'd it go, superstars?" he asked, with arms open wide.

"I don't want to talk about it," growled Romeo.

Andrew looked at the three of them slumping

toward the car. "That good, huh?" he asked. Lou and Gary shrugged listlessly.

Romeo spun around to address everyone once and for all. "Look, I'm tired, okay?" he said. "I'm the one who's been driving the past two days straight," he reminded them. "Let me just take a nap and we'll deal with it later."

With that, he climbed in the car and slammed the door. He grabbed his hat off the seat and tilted it over his head. Adjusting the seat back, he closed his eyes. It was nap time.

Lou, Gary, and Andrew huddled outside the building. "All this way and he's just giving up?" Louis said, bewildered.

"Not like the Ro," agreed Gary. His brother was the most determined person he knew. When he wanted something, he didn't give up until he got it.

Louis thought a moment. "I've got an idea," he said, breaking into a run toward the building. "I better go with you," Gary yelled. "Someone has to figure out the other half of your idea."

He threw Andrew his duffel bag. "Hey, Andrew,"

he said. "Keep an eye on Romeo." The black-clad cow-boy glanced toward the car.

Up at Joe Blanchard's office, his assistant entered, carrying a notebook full of papers. "The press conference is at six," said the long-haired young man, "and we still need an opening act for JoJo."

Joe took a break from his phone call to respond. "I know, I know," he said. "I'm working on it."

The office door opened and Louis and Gary stepped inside. Behind them, his other assistant apolo-gized. "I'm sorry, sir, they just . . ." she gestured at them helplessly. She gave a toss of her long, black hair.

"Mr. Blanchard," Lou said. "I'm Louis Miller."

Joe looked up, and waved away his assistant. "They're okay," he said. "I met you and Ro on the golf course in Seattle," he said, pointing to Lou.

"Exactly," said Lou, relieved that he remembered. He looked at all the gold records lining the wall.

"Good to see you again," Joe said with a nod.

Gary sprang forth impatiently. "This is a beautiful moment and all," he said, putting his elbows on Joe's desk, "but why'd you blow Romeo off?"

Joe raised his eyebrows. "Blow him off?!" he said, surprised. "I told him he could perform as the opening act for JoJo tonight." He looked at Gary, and then at Lou.

"And he turned that down?" asked Louis, shocked. Was Romeo crazy?

"Yeah," Joe nodded, "because I need a solo artist. And Ro said the only way he plays . . ." — He gestured toward the two of them. — ". . . is with his band." Lou and Gary looked at each other in disbelief.

Louis took a step back. "Man, this is Romeo's dream," he said. "And he gave it up for us."

It was a lot to take in. Romeo had been handed the opportunity of a lifetime: opening for a hot music star, in front of an audience of thousands. It had been Ro who had pushed them to make this journey, traveling two days and risking Percy's anger.

And now he was giving it all up because he didn't want his family to get left out.

Gary and Louis left the office in shock.

CHAPTER 12

BUSTED

At the Miller home, Bobby sat gurgling in his infant seat, while Ashley, Myra, Jodi, and Hacksaw buzzed around him. Ashley and Myra were sorting stacks of Bobby's head shots. Hacksaw paced and talked on his cell. Jodi took her phone over to the far side of the kitchen, trying to be heard above the noise.

"Look, all I'm saying is, Bobby Miller is in high demand," she said. "So it would be in your best interest to consider him. . . ."

Just then, they heard the crunch of footsteps on the pavement outside, and the sound of a turning doorknob. The kitchen door swung open. It was Angeline.

Myra shot Jodi a look of panic, and Jodi got off

the phone in a hurry. Her stepmother looked at the kitchen, horrified.

All around her, Bobby's face was plastered on ads for Crandall's Baby Food, and Stack-a-Block Toys. Head shots of Bobby dotted the walls of the kitchen and living room. Hacksaw was in the background, talking on his cell and writing on a notepad.

Angeline looked at Jodi in dismay. "Jodi," she said, putting down her purse. "What are you doing?"

"I'm, uh, um . . ." Jodi stumbled, trying to think fast. "I'm launching the newest Miller star!" she said with shaky bravado. "Where's Dad?" she gulped.

She feared his reaction most of all. Though Percy was a fair and loving father, he was not afraid to dole out punishment.

"He's outside, getting the bags," said Angeline. She went to unstrap Bobby from his infant seat. "What is going on?" she asked.

Ashley knew there was about to be a showdown, and she didn't want to be around for it. She whispered to Myra, "How's this going to work out?" Myra looked at Angeline's angry face, and knew things were bad. Ang almost never lost her cool.

"We don't really need to see," said Myra, motioning to Ashley. They started to slide toward the back door.

"Oh, no, no, no, no, no," Angeline said, stopping Ashley and Myra. "You two wait right here." She wanted Percy to see the entire operation.

"Staying right here, Ang," Myra said, resigned.

"Not moving a muscle." Ashley sighed, knowing they were trapped. She and Myra were involved now, too.

Angeline went up to the baby food poster, examining a three-foot image of Bobby's face. "How could you do this without telling us?" she demanded. He wasn't even old enough to walk! Ang shook her head, exasperated.

"It's my new career!" announced Jodi, with a nervous smile. She tried out her new sales skills on her stepmother. "I think I have a real gift for personal management," she confided.

Angeline was furious. "He's not. Yet. A. Year. Old," she said, drawing out the words for emphasis.

"You guys are shutting this down. *Now.*" Jodi was deflated. So much for her new career.

Hacksaw darted by on this cell phone. "I kept telling her that," he said to Angeline. He took his cell to the other end of the kitchen, dialing quickly. "Cindy, it's Hacksaw," he said in a low voice. "What's baby Mercy doin' tomorrow?"

Jodi glared at him. Hacksaw looked from Jodi to Angeline, realizing his mistake. "I'll call you back," he said, shrinking under Jodi's gaze.

Myra, Ashley, and Jodi started taking Bobby's photographs down. Outside, they heard the sound of luggage wheels. If Angie was this mad, what would Percy say?

Lou and Gary left Joe's office in a daze. JoJo was known for putting on an awesome show, and opening for her would put any musician on the map. But Romeo had turned it down because his brothers would be left out.

The two of them rode down in the elevator in silence, lost in their own thoughts.

Lou recalled the time Romeo had entered a local rap-off contest without telling anyone. When the family learned about the event, they were convinced Romeo was trying to launch a solo career. Everyone was upset.

But they'd shown up at the rap-off anyway, determined to support Romeo. Unable to take the pressure, Ro lost his nerve in front of the bloodthirsty crowd. Luckily, Gary, Lou, and Jodi were there to help him out. They rushed on stage and put on a great show.

Afterward, Ro explained he'd never wanted to be a solo act. He'd entered the contest as a personal challenge, and he was grateful his family had shown up to help. Afterward, Louis felt bad that he'd ever doubted Ro's loyalty.

Besides being devoted to the band, Ro had also been loyal to Lou personally. Ever since he'd come to live with the Millers, Ro had watched out for Lou. They had shared bunk beds, lockers, even underwear (but not on purpose!).

So how could he let his brother pass up a chance like this?

On the elevator ride, Gary also had time to think.

During rehearsals, Ro was always pushing the band to work harder. Practicing their songs over and over took time Gary wasn't always willing to give. Ro was the one who was most committed to music.

Gary had other schemes to hatch, like opening a chain of gourmet lemonade stands, or starting an Internet business. In fact, he was just beginning to build his financial empire. He liked to dream about going platinum, but was that mostly a fantasy about getting rich?

When the elevator doors opened with a thud, Gary and Lou both started talking at once. "We need to talk to Joe right away . . . ?" Lou said, at the same time Gary said, "We can't let Ro back out now. . . ?"

They laughed and Lou said, "Let's start over. What are we doing, standing in Ro's way?" asked Lou. "We can't let him make this choice. It's just, like, not an option."

"Yeah," agreed Gary. "He's *got* to do the show tonight."

He thought about the fan mail they got on their Web site. Three quarters of it was for Ro — he was the one who brought in the crowds. Of all of them, Ro was the true inheritor of their father's musical talent.

"So should we . . . ?" began Lou again.

"Yup," said Gary, pushing the elevator button.

They had to see Joe and tell him Ro would do the show tonight after all. Ro had turned the show down because of Lou and Gary, but his brothers hadn't known about it. Once Joe found out Lou and Gary *wanted* Ro to perform, he'd be thrilled.

If it wasn't already too late.

The elevator seemed to take forever as different characters came and left: a woman with a red cape and a Chihuahua, a businessman in a pinstripe suit, a pair of skinhead men carrying guitar cases.

When they got back up to the thirty-second floor, they headed straight to Joe Blanchard's office. His female assistant, a pretty girl with long, dark hair, was bustling around her desk. She groaned when she saw them.

"Not you two again." She sighed. Last time they'd practically bulldozed their way in to see Joe. "What now?" she asked wearily.

"We need to see Mr. Blanchard again," said Lou. "It's important, we swear."

"Sorry," she said. "He's tied up in an important call to Tokyo. You'll have to wait."

"There isn't time to wait," said Lou impatiently. Joe might be agreeing to book some other band at this very moment!

"Yeah," agreed Gary. "This is kind of like life or death."

"Sorry, guys. This time he really can't be disturbed. I mean it." She pointed to a couple of chairs outside his office. "You can wait here until he's through. But I don't know when that will be." She shrugged.

Lou and Gary sighed and slumped into the chairs she offered them. This could take forever, they realized. While she took calls and made notes in the calendar in front of her, she kept an eye on them. This time she wasn't taking any chances.

Then Gary had an idea.

"I'm going to the bathroom," he announced to Lou. He headed toward the rest room, but turned down the hall instead. Peeking into every window, he finally saw an empty conference room. There was a phone inside, and he used it to call Joe's assistant.

"There's a package in the conference room for Joe," he said, disguising his voice. "New shipment of CDs," he added.

She sighed and started down the hall to the conference room. Gary leaped into the bathroom, then bolted out again when the coast was clear. "Come on," he said to Lou when he returned, and they dove for the door of Joe's office.

When they busted inside, Joe was talking on his headset while his other assistant sorted through piles of CDs. Lou and Gary filed in and sat down on chairs opposite Joe. The young male assistant just looked at them, and brushed back his long hair.

"The Asia tour was a sellout," Joe was saying. "I just hope we have the same success in Europe." When he saw Lou and Gary, he said, "Hold on a minute." Looking from Lou to Gary, he said, "Guys?"

"Romeo's going to perform for you tonight at the Greek Theater," announced Lou. "Count on it."

His female assistant came into the room and threw an exasperated look at Lou and Gary. "Joe, Big Ben is on line two. He wants to know if you still need him to open for JoJo tonight."

Joe looked at Lou and Gary. "Can you give me your word about Romeo?" Joe asked. "If not, I'll have to book Big Ben."

Lou hesitated for a half second. Romeo hadn't, in fact, actually agreed to doing the show. Hopefully, Lou and Gary would be able to talk him into it. In the meantime, Joe needed to know *right now* — otherwise he'd book the other rapper.

"Yes," said Louis firmly. "He's totally psyched."

"Okay," said Joe. To his assistant, he said, "Tell Ben we've already got someone." He looked at Lou and Gary and said, "Have Romeo get up here to see me immediately."

"Right away," promised Lou. He looked at Gary — they were just in time! A minute later, and Joe would have booked someone else.

"Now, gentlemen, you'll have to excuse me," he said with a smile. He adjusted his headset to continue his other conversation.

Closing the door to Joe's office, the boys sighed with relief. They ran to the elevator and pushed the button over and over. "Come on, open up, open up," beseeched Lou impatiently.

"After all this, what if Ro doesn't agree to do the show?" asked Gary. "You know how stubborn he is."

"Then we're in deep trouble," agreed Lou. "To tell you the truth, I hadn't really gotten that far."

The elevator finally opened with a *ding*. They knocked fists, grateful they'd been able to convince Joe.

Now all they had to do was convince Romeo.

Louis and Gary bolted down the steps of the building and over to the car. They leaned in the window and looked at Ro. "Come on, man, wake up," said Gary. Ro was stretched out sleeping in the front seat, his hat over his eyes.

"Joe told us everything," said Lou. Ro stirred awake, annoyed at being disturbed. Why couldn't his brothers leave him alone?

Romeo shook his head stubbornly. "I told you, I don't wanna talk about it," he mumbled. He shut his eyes to show he was still asleep.

Louis opened the door to the driver's seat and sat down. "Well, we do," he said. "So scoot over." Ro grudgingly sat up, but his eyes remained closed.

"Romeo," said Lou. "You have to go on tonight." He said this in a firm, won't-take-no-for-an-answer voice. "You have wanted this since I moved in."

Louis recalled Romeo as a kid in junior high, rapping on the school bus, the basketball court — even in the swimming pool. As long as he had known his brother, he'd had a mike in his hand, spilling out rhymes faster than he could write them down.

"Even before," insisted Gary. "You would sing to Mom any song that was on the radio." Ro's face softened at the memory of her. It was true, he had been performing ever since he was old enough to walk.

"You've always talked about 'our' time," pressed Louis, using Ro's own words. "How our time would come and we would blow up," he said passionately. "How our time would come, and the world would hear our music."

Ro turned to him. "That's it, Lou," he said. "*Our* music. It's always been about that for me," he explained. "You guys have always been behind me. No matter what I thought of you, you guys were there for me," he said simply. "We're a team."

"We are," said Gary. "We're Team Miller."

"And we always will be," stressed Lou. "But you wanted this more than me, Ro," he said. "When I'm out of high school, I'm done."

"What?" said Ro. It never occurred to Ro that Lou might have other plans for his life. He'd always assumed they'd all stick with the band as long as their success lasted.

"Yeah," said Louis, with a shrug. "I want to be an airline pilot."

"Say WHAT?" Ro squeaked, not believing his ears. When had Lou come up with that one? Though come to think of it, he did always love plane trips.

"Think about it," Lou said dreamily. "Fly around, see the world, meet girls, wear a uniform," he said. "Girls love guys who wear uniforms," he informed Ro.

Ro had to admit he had a point — he always met girls in his basketball duds. "I can't disagree with that," he said, clinking fists with Lou.

"And I'm heading to video games," said Gary proudly.

Ro turned to face him. "You're going to play video games for a living?" he said skeptically.

"No way," said Gary, waving his hand. "I'm

going to *own* them. They sell way more than albums," he explained. Ro nodded. Gary always had grand schemes for making money.

Lou looked at his brother. "So what do you want to do, Ro? Dad always said that we each have a path to follow." Ro thought about Percy, encouraging him to be his own person.

"Yeah," said Gary, looking at Ro. "So go follow yours."

Ro looked at Lou and Gary — they were serious. He smiled at both of them, realizing the gift he'd been given. They wanted him to take the spotlight even if it meant leaving them behind.

They insisted they had other plans, but Romeo knew they were disappointed. They had all been looking forward to performing for Joe, and getting a shot at the big-time.

Yet here they were, pushing him to do it without them.

Now *that* was love.

Andrew looked into the car window. He looked at Gary, who smiled and gave him a meaningful nod.

He smiled back, looking at all three of them. Ro's grin could only mean one thing.

Walking away from the car, Andrew's fingers moved over his cell phone. "Mr. Miller, you are not going to believe this, sir," he began. "But you have to get yourself to Los Angeles. Pronto."

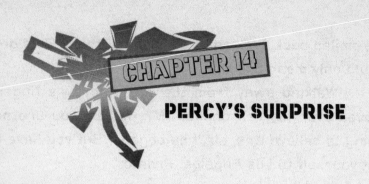

CHAPTER 14

PERCY'S SURPRISE

As Percy hauled the bags into the house, everyone froze. Now they were *really* in trouble. Percy wouldn't be happy to see what had gone on behind his back — and now, there was no hiding it.

Just as he wheeled the suitcases in, his cell phone rang. Myra, Ashley, and Jodi watched as he listened and raised his eyebrows. "You're kidding me," he said, shaking his head. "Alright, later." He folded up his phone and put it back in his white jacket.

Looking around the kitchen, he saw what was left of the Miller Talent Agency: giant ads for Crandall's Baby Food and Stack-a-Blocks, featuring a smiling Bobby. There were still a few head shots plastered on the kitchen cabinets.

He put his hands on his hips. "So this is what happens when parents leave their kids alone?" he demanded angrily. Jodi, Myra, and Ashley looked down at the floor, ashamed.

Jodi kept her head down, waiting for her father's speech on honesty and responsibility. Instead, Percy cleared his throat. "Alright. Everybody in the car," he ordered. "We're going to the airport."

Everyone looked at each other, baffled. The airport?! What kind of punishment did he have in mind? Even Angeline was stumped. "Um, honey?" she asked. "What's going on?"

But Percy had already headed back out the door to the family car. Shrugging, they followed him outside.

They knew better than to disobey orders.

The Greek Theater was sold out that night. Thousands of JoJo fans squirmed in their seats, psyched to see the beloved music star.

Backstage, Romeo paced around, sneaking peeks at the audience. He had performed for crowds of several hundred people — not several *thousand* people. All three tiers of the stadium were bulging with bodies, and the noise was deafening.

Come to think of it, he hadn't even *been* to an arena this size before, much less played in one. The clubs they played in tended to be hip night spots — but they weren't huge.

This place was a different story.

Joe Blanchard came by to wish him good luck. He looked sharp in a pink shirt, his backstage pass on a cord around his neck. As usual, he wore a headset. "So, Romeo," he said. "Are you ready?"

Romeo fidgeted with his wristband. "Always," he said, trying to act like singing in front of ten thousand people was no big deal.

"Alright, kid," said Joe, laughing at Ro's enthusiasm. "Good luck. Just go out there and do what you do," he advised. "If the audience responds, your world changes," Joe said simply. "Good luck, Ro."

Talk about *pressure*.

Romeo took off his baseball cap and put it back on again. His throat was dry and his heart was pounding. Performing without the band would be hard enough — but knowing what depended on his performance made it even harder.

This was more than a show — it was the audition of a lifetime. Never before had so much rested on one of Ro's concerts.

He had thought he had the stuff. Now, looking out at the endless wall of people, he wasn't so sure. Gary and Lou came up next to him and gawked at the sea of people.

"Wow, Ro," said Gary, "I don't think I've ever seen so many people in an audience." The three tiers of the arena were packed to the rafters.

Louis poked Gary. "Dude," he scolded him. "Don't make him more nervous than he looks." At this moment, he wouldn't trade places with Romeo. The crowd was daunting.

Behind them, they heard a female voice. "How's it looking out there?" the girl said. They spun around and saw a gorgeous teenage girl with streaked reddish-blond hair and beautiful green eyes. "You're Romeo, right?" she asked.

Louis did a double take. "JoJo?" he asked, amazed. They had seen her face before on television, but she was even cuter in person. In her bright orange jacket and big hoop earrings, she seemed friendly and relaxed.

She looked at all of them and smiled, extending her hand to Romeo. Peeking out of her jacket was a diamond studded nameplate necklace that said Jo.

Automatically, Louis took out his camera and snapped a picture of her. Ro gave him an exasperated look — couldn't Louis be cool? Celebrities hated that stuff.

But JoJo didn't seem to mind at all. "Hey," said Romeo, grasping her hand eagerly. "Hey," she said. "You totally saved the day!" Her big eyes widened as she said this.

Romeo smiled and shrugged. "I'm just happy to be here," he said.

"You deserve it," JoJo said warmly. "Joe played me some of your stuff and it's really good."

Ro beamed at the compliment. "Thank you," he

said. JoJo was a rising pop star, known for her dance-able party tunes. Her encouragement was flattering.

"Are you nervous?" she asked.

"Me?" asked Ro, with a short laugh. "Nah, not at all," he said, waving his hand dismissively. His eyes met Gary's and his bravado collapsed. "Yeah, I am," he admitted.

"I thought so," she said with a sympathetic chuckle. "Just take some deep breaths, go out there, and do your thing," she said. "The crowd's going to love it."

A blond woman with a clipboard came by and handed Romeo a microphone. She was the stage manager, he realized. "They're going to announce you in two minutes, Romeo," she said. "Okay?"

"Thank you, " Ro said, taking the mike. Suddenly, it felt like an unfamiliar object.

"Alright," said JoJo, taking a few steps back. "Go out there and get 'em. I'm going to be in the wings watching, so I'll see you all after the show." She waved and Romeo and Lou watched her walk away. Her long hair swayed behind her as she moved.

"Man, she is *so hot*," raved Lou. Ro and Gary smiled in agreement.

As they watched her disappear around a corner, Ro heard a deep voice coming from behind him.

"Romeo . . ." The boys turned around and gasped in disbelief.

Standing right in front of them was Percy.

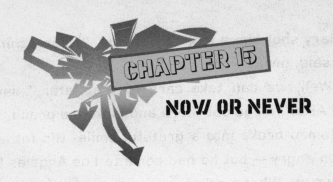

CHAPTER 15

NOW OR NEVER

"We're dead," Ro informed his brothers.

"Uh-oh," said Gary.

They looked up at their father, massive in his white linen jacket and blue baseball cap that said TEAM RESPECT. He folded his arms in front of him, looking at each brother.

"You guys are in so much trouble," he said, in a serious voice. The boys looked down at the floor. His timing couldn't have been worse.

Show time was in thirty seconds. Would his father even allow him to perform?

Romeo's body twitched as he rushed to defend himself. "Look," he said. "You know, it was Gary's idea...." he started to ramble.

Gary shot him a look of outrage. "I don't *think* so," he said, giving Romeo a shove.

"Well, we can take care of that later," said Percy. "After you go out there and make me proud."

Romeo broke into a grateful smile. His father had been angry — but he had come to Los Angeles to cheer him on. What a relief!

Lou and Gary exchanged glances. Percy was on board with the concert — that was all that mattered. Down the hall they heard familiar voices, laughter, and stroller wheels.

Angeline, Bobby, Jodi, Hacksaw, Myra, and Ashley rushed up to them excitedly. Crowding around Romeo, Jodi squeezed his arm, and Myra gave him a hug. Ashley blew him a kiss, and Hacksaw stretched out his hand for a high five.

Coming up to Percy, Angeline gave him a kiss. She was glad he'd been able to put aside his anger to support his son. She knew how much Romeo needed him right now.

Bobby pounded the stroller tray, as if he wanted to congratulate Ro, too. Romeo reached down to his baby brother, clinking his tiny fist with his own.

An announcement blasted over the loudspeaker. "And now, ladies and gentlemen, Los Angeles is very proud to present Seattle's own . . . ROMEO MILLER!" Everyone around Romeo shrieked.

The crowd swelled with applause, and Romeo's gang clapped and whistled. "I can't believe it!" squealed Ashley. Romeo looked at his family. It was now or never.

Ro looked up at his father with uncertainty. He had wanted this so badly — now it was here. Was he up to the challenge?

Percy looked at him evenly and nodded, as if to say, "Yes. You can do it." Ro realized he hadn't asked the question out loud. As usual, his father had read his mind, knowing what Ro needed, before he even knew it himself.

Taking a deep breath, Ro collected the last of the high fives and sprinted to the stage. It seemed like he floated there. He looked back at Percy, who gave him one last nod of encouragement.

And all at once, he was standing in front of a gigantic crowd, facing a sea of faces that seemed to stretch out for miles in front of him. It was the moment he'd been waiting for all of his life.

Yikes.

Ro clutched the mike and brought it up to his mouth. For a second, it seemed like no words would come out. And then, they came all at once. Ro's dream was there — all he had to do was grab it.

He broke into his first song, waving his hand above his head in time to the beat.

You know, I'm feeling you, you need
To be my girl, can't keep it inside
Another day, like the sound of the
Month of May —

As he moved, beams of light danced around him. The giant arena dwarfed Romeo, but he took command of the stage with an almost superhuman energy. He leaped, strolled, strutted, and swayed, captivating the audience with his lightning-quick moves.

He used his fingers to pantomime a beating heart, butterflies in his stomach, and other symptoms of a serious crush. Thousands of fans waved their arms along with him. He sang:

I get nervous, my
Heart skips a beat, I think its
Time we should meet

Backstage, his crew was grooving to the music. Ashley snapped her fingers and swiveled her hips, Myra swayed and shook her long blond curls, Lou and Gary nodded and played imaginary instruments. Percy and Ang danced hand-to-hand.

Ro brought the energy up now, singing his heart out to everyone in the audience.

Guess that's
Why I hesitated, but I know we can
Make it, girl, hope you feel the
Same way I do, from the top of the
Grandstands, I'm going for you. . . .

The crowd went nuts. Wild cheers, hooting, and foot-stomping followed. Ro took a breath and wiped his brow. In front of him was an audience of thousands, begging for more.

Catching his breath for a moment, Ro looked back at his family. Like the audience, they were cheering and clapping. They looked at Ro adoringly, as if to say, "See? You did it! We knew you could!"

Ro smiled and gave them a thumbs-up. It was great to know that his family was just a few feet behind him.

In fact, they were behind him all the way.